MISS CAPRICE

ST. GEORGE RATHBORNE

1st WORLD LIBRARY
Literary Society

Miss Caprice

St. George Rathborne

© 1st World Library, 2009
PO Box 2211
Fairfield, IA 52556
www.1stworldlibrary.com
First Edition

LCCN: 2009923389

Softcover ISBN: 978-1-4218-8837-8
Hardcover ISBN: 978-1-4218-8936-8
eBook ISBN: 978-1-4218-8738-8

Purchase *"Miss Caprice"*
as a traditional bound book at:
www.1stWorldLibrary.com/purchase.asp?ISBN=978-1-4218-8837-8

1st World Library is a literary, educational organization
dedicated to:

- Creating a free internet library of downloadable ebooks

- Hosting writing competitions and offering book publishing scholarships.

Interested in more 1st World Library books? contact:
literacy@1stworldlibrary.com
Check us out at: www.1stworldlibrary.com

1ˢᵗ World Library Literary Society

Giving Back to the World

"If you want to work on the core problem, it's early school literacy."

- James Barksdale, former CEO of Netscape

"No skill is more crucial to the future of a child, or to a democratic and prosperous society, than literacy."

- Los Angeles Times

"Literacy... means far more than learning how to read and write... The aim is to transmit... knowledge and promote social participation."

- UNESCO

"Literacy is not a luxury, it is a right and a responsibility. If our world is to meet the challenges of the twenty-first century we must harness the energy and creativity of all our citizens."

- President Bill Clinton

"Parents should be encouraged to read to their children, and teachers should be equipped with all available techniques for teaching literacy, so the varying needs and capacities of individual kids can be taken into account."

- Hugh Mackay

CHAPTER I

"COWARD!"

A little party of tourists might be seen one lovely day in January, on the hill back of the city of Valetta, on that gem of Mediterranean islands, Great Britain's Malta.

The air is as clear as a bell, and the scene is certainly one to charm the senses, with the blue Mediterranean, dotted with sails, a hazy line far, far away that may be the coast of Africa, the double harbor below, one known as Quarantine, where general trade is done, the other, Great Harbor, being devoted to government vessels.

Quaint indeed is the appearance of the Maltese city that rests mostly upon the side of the hill under the fortifications, a second Quebec as it were.

The streets are, some of them, very steep, the houses, built of limestone, generally three stories in height, with a flat roof that answers the same purpose as the Spanish or Mexican *azotea.*

Valetta has three city gates, one the Porta Reale, through which our little tourist group came to reach their present position, leads to the country; the Porta Marsamuscetto to the general harbor where lie craft of all nations, while the government harbor is reached by means of the Marina gate.

Thus they hold to many of the ways of Moorish and Mohammedan countries.

The fortifications of limestone are massive—England has a second Gibraltar here.

In general, the Maltese speak a language not unlike the Arabic, though English and Italian are used in trade.

They are a swarthy, robust, fearless people, strong in their loves and hates, and the vendetta has been known to exist here just as fiercely as in its native home of Corsica.

Many dress in the costume of the Franks, but the native garb is still worn by the lower classes, and is a picturesque sight, such as we see upon the stage.

It consists of a long bag made of wool, and dyed various colors, making a cap such as is worn by the sailors in stage scenes like the "Pirates of Penzance."

The top part of this is used for a purse, or forms a receptacle for any small articles the wearer desires to carry.

A short, loose pantaloon, to the knee, which leaves the lower leg bare, is confined at the waist by a girdle or sash of colored cotton or silk. Then there is worn a cotton shirt, with a short, loose vest, or waistcoat, as they were formerly known, covering the same; the latter often ornamented with rows of silver buttons, quarter-dollars, or English shillings.

As to the ladies of Malta, their costume is very odd, and reminds one somewhat of Spain. In part, it consists of a black silk petticoat, bound round the waist, over a body of some other kind of silk or print which is called the *half onuella*. The upper part, the *onuella*, of the same material, is drawn into neat gathers for the length of a foot about the center of one of the outer seams. In the seam of one of the remaining divisions is inclosed a piece of whalebone, which is drawn over the head, and forms a perfect arch, leaving the head and neck bare.

As may be expected, it requires much practice to wear such a dress gracefully. Many of the best ladies of Valetta now get their fashions direct from Paris—so the world moves.

The little party of tourists have ascended the hill for the purpose of obtaining the glorious view referred to, and at the same time whiling away a few hours of time, for their stay at the Island of Malta has not been of their choosing, a peculiar accident causing the steamer on which they were taking passage to put in here for some necessary repairs.

The tourists are five in number, and a very brief description will give the reader an idea as to their identity, leaving individual peculiarities to be developed as our story progresses.

Probably the one that would attract the attention of a stranger first would be the young lady with the peach-bloom complexion and sunny blue eyes, whose figure is so stylish, and whose rather haughty manner bespeaks proud English blood.

There is another female, whom the young lady calls Aunt Gwen, and as a specimen of a man-female she certainly takes the premium, being tall, angular, yet muscular, and with a face that is rather Napoleonic in its cast. A born diplomat, and never so happy as when engaged in a broil or a scene of some sort, they have given this Yankee aunt of Lady Ruth the name of Gwendolin Makepeace. And as she has an appendage somewhere, known as a husband, her final appellation is Sharpe, which somehow suits her best of all.

Aunt Gwen is a character to be watched, and bound to bob up serenely, with the most amazing assurance, at unexpected times.

Then there is Sharpe, her worse half, a small gentleman over whom she towers, and of whom she is secretly fond in her way, though she tyrannizes him dreadfully.

Near him may be seen a young American, whom they have somehow dubbed "Doctor Chicago," because he is a medical student hailing from that wonderful city, by name John Alexander Craig. Among his friends he is simply Aleck. His manner is buoyant, and he looks like an overgrown boy, but his record thus far proves his brain to contain that which will some day cause him to forge ahead.

No one knows why Craig is abroad. That he has some mission besides a tour for health and sight-seeing, several little things have proved.

There is another member of the group, a gentleman of sturdy build, with a handsome face, whose ruddy tint suggests the English officer, even without the flowing whiskers.

Colonel Lionel Blunt has seen much service in India and around Cape Colony. He gained an enviable reputation for deeds of valor, and is disposed to look upon our friend from Chicago as an amiable boy, though after seeing how they rush things out in that Western metropolis he may have occasional qualms of fear lest this young doctor finally reach the goal for which both are aiming. That goal, any one can see, is the favor of the bright English girl whom fate has thrown in their way. Perhaps it is not all fate, since Colonel

Lionel has recently crossed the States coming from India, and seems to pursue Lady Ruth with singular pertinacity.

Others are present, one a Maltese gentleman, the proprietor of a select club-house, where the garrison officers fence and engage in gymnastics, but Signor Giovani is not of our party.

There are also several commissionaires or guides, at five francs a day, for one cannot move at Malta without being attended, and it is wise to engage one cicerone to keep the rest of his tribe at bay.

Thus, on the hill above the singular Maltese city of Valetta, our story opens.

Aunt Gwen is sweeping a field-glass around, and emphasizing her admiration of the picturesque scene with various phrases that would immediately give her away as a Western Yankee.

Lady Ruth, with an admirer on each side, looks a trifle tired, or, it may be, bored.

She may be planning some innocent little scheme, such as girls are wont to indulge in when they have a superfluity of beaus, in order to extract some amusement from the situation, even if it come under the head of "cruelty to animals."

Philander Sharpe, with his hands under the tails of his long coat, and his glasses pushed up on his forehead, is a study for a painter.

He was once a professor in a Western college, and with his smooth face, hair reached up from his high forehead, standing collar, and general dignified air, is no mean-looking figure, though dwarfed into insignificance by the side of his spouse, the wonderful Aunt Gwen.

The conversation runs upon what lies there before them, and an animated discussion arises as to the possibility of a foreign enemy ever being able to successfully assault this second Gibraltar of the Mediterranean.

Of course, the young American is enthusiastic, and has unbounded faith in the new White Squadron to accomplish anything, while, on the other hand, the British officer, like most of his class, believes that John Bull is invincible on land or wave. Of course, the young man from Chicago disputes the point, and energetically contends that no nation is superior to the Republic, or that any flag can be more desperately defended than "Old Glory."

And right in the midst of the heated discussion Lady Ruth smiles, as though she has suddenly hit upon an idea at last— an idea that offers a solution to the problem that has been perplexing her of late, concerning the courage of these rival admirers.

She turns to the American, and smiles sweetly.

"Doctor, you speak of your countrymen being brave; will you prove it?" is what she says.

The young man turns a trifle red.

"I beg your pardon. In speaking of Americans I did not intend to sound my own praises. Personally, I never claimed more than the average amount of boldness, though I don't know that I was ever called a coward."

His manner is modest, but the young girl with English ideas

St. George Rathborne

chooses to look upon his words with suspicion.

"Doctor Chicago must not take water. I have surely understood him to be a regular fire-eater—that all Chicago has rung with his escapades," says the colonel of Royal Engineers, sneeringly.

"Nonsense! But, Lady Ruth, you spoke of my proving something—what can I do for you?"

"Look!"

She extends a shapely arm. Her finger points to a white flower growing out upon the face of the precipice beside them.

"Do you see that flower?" she asks.

"I do," he replies, calmly.

"I would like to possess it."

The young man looks down. A fall means instant death, and it would be impossible for even an experienced Alpine traveler to pass along the face of the rock in safety.

"I see no means of reaching the flower, or I assure you I would gladly secure it for you."

"Ah! but a bold man would climb out there."

"Pardon—he would be a fool—his life would pay the penalty for a pretty girl's whim. Unfortunately, perhaps, my life is too precious to some one other than myself, to admit of the sacrifice. I am willing to do much for Lady Ruth, but I decline to be made a fool of."

"Well spoken," begins the professor.

"Philander!" exclaims his spouse, and the little man draws in his head very much after the style of a tortoise.

"Coward!"

The English girl is sorry as soon as the low word leaves her lips. No one hears it but the young doctor, for the attention of all the others is at that time directed elsewhere.

This time the object of her scorn does not flush, but turns very white, as he looks her steadily in the eyes.

"I am sorry you have such a poor opinion of me, Lady Ruth. I make no apologies, save the one that my life is too valuable —to others, to myself—to throw it away at the mere caprice of a girl."

"There is a gentleman who finds a way to accomplish what he wants. Take a lesson from him, Doctor Chicago," she says.

Colonel Lionel has noticed a long pole near by, in the end of which is a cleft. This he has secured, and, by crawling as far as is safe along the face of the rock, he is enabled to just reach the flower.

After a number of ineffectual lunges he succeeds in clutching the coveted article in the cleft of the pole, and draws it toward him.

A moment later he presents the flower to Lady Ruth, with a smile and a bow.

"No English lady ever expressed a wish that a British officer did not feel bound in honor to grant," he says.

The girl thanks him, and then says:

"After all, the flower was prettier at a distance than when in my hands."

Colonel Lionel hardly knows whether he has made such a huge advance over his rival after all.

The afternoon sun is waning.

"We must go down," declares Aunt Gwen.

"One more look around and I am ready," says Lady Ruth.

Already she is sorry for her cruel words. Like the best of women, she can wound at one moment and be contrite the next. She finds an opportunity a minute later, when the colonel lingers to get the shawl she—perhaps purposely—left behind, to say in a low tone:

"I was cruel—forgive me—forget that foolish word," and while what she utters gives him a pleasurable feeling, and brings the color into his set face, he only smiles, as he answers:

"Willingly, Lady Ruth. I did not believe you could mean it."

Then, as the colonel bustles up, the subject is tabooed, and the party of tourists proceed down the steep street leading to the Hotel Imperial.

CHAPTER II

A DEADLY ENCOUNTER

The scene, so peaceful, so picturesque, is rudely broken in upon by a clamor so strange and awful that the blood is chilled in the listeners' veins. Cries are heard down the steep street; cries that indicate alarm, even terror; cries that proceed from children, women, ay, and strong men, too.

Our party comes to a halt midway between the brow of the hill and the base. On either side tall houses, the declivity ending only at the water. It is a bustling street at all hours, with loungers, business men, women going to and returning from market, and children playing as children do the world over, in the dirt.

"What can it mean?" says Lady Ruth, as she looks breathlessly down the street.

No one in their party can explain the cause of the excitement. They see people running madly this way and that, as if panic-stricken.

"By Jove! it must be a fire!" suggests the colonel, twirling his whiskers.

St. George Rathborne

"Nonsense! we should see the smoke," declares sensible Aunt Gwen.

"You are right; it is something more than a fire. Those people are almost crazed. I've seen such a sight in Chicago, when a wild Texan steer got loose and tossed things right and left," asserts the medical student.

"That's what's the matter. See! they point at something as they run! Look out for the bull!" cries Philander.

Thus, in watching for a bulky frame to appear, they fail to notice the actual cause of the disturbance.

The street is almost deserted, save where people begin to reappear below, as though the danger were past, to reappear and shout afresh as they wave their arms.

Some one is shouting close to them now. They turn their heads and behold the crowd of commissionaires dashing headlong for the shelter of adjacent houses, and acting like crazy men.

It is Signor Giovani who shouts, first in Arabic, then in Italian, and finally in English. They hear him now, and no wonder the blood runs cold in their veins—it is a cry to alarm the boldest warrior on earth.

"Mad dog! Run, signors!—save the ladies! To the houses, or you are lost!"

That is what the old fencing-master of Malta shouts while he retreats. It causes them to turn their heads, and what do they see? Advancing up the middle of the inclined street, turning aside for neither king nor peasant, comes a great gaunt beast, his square head wagging from side to side, his eyes blood-shot, and the foam dropping from his open jaws.

Heavens! What a spectacle to rivet one with horror to the spot. Fortunately there are some people of action present.

Aunt Gwen clutches her *infant* by the shoulder, and drags him along in the direction of the nearest house.

"Run, Philander, or you're a goner! It's worse than snake poison, the bite of a mad dog is. Haven't I seen a bitten man so furious that it required six to hold him down? Faster, professor! on your life!"

With that iron grip on his shoulder poor Philander's feet barely touch the ground as he is whirled through space, and the dog, mad or not, that overtakes Aunt Gwen and her infant must be a rapid traveler, indeed. Thus they reach a house, and in another minute reappear upon a balcony, to witness a scene they will never forget.

Lady Ruth, though naturally quivering with excitement, has plenty of cavaliers to hurry her to a place of safety. Besides, after that one first shock, she shows more grit than might have been expected of her.

She allows herself to be hurried along. A strong hand grasps each arm; and if every one in the path of the mad brute were as well attended, there would be little cause for anxiety or alarm.

Now they have reached a house, and safety is assured, for the hospitable door stands open to welcome them.

Already a number have preceded them, for they seem to be the last in the vicinity.

Just as they arrive, the colonel, who appears intensely excited, is saying, hoarsely:

"Enter quickly, I beg, Lady Ruth."

She turns her head in curiosity for one last look, impelled by an unknown power—turns, and is at once petrified by what she sees.

They notice the look of horror on her lovely face, and instinctively guessing, also cast a glance in the direction where last the savage brute was seen.

He has continued to advance in the interim, and is now quite close, though not moving out of the straight line in the center of the street—a repulsive looking object truly, and enough to horrify the bravest.

Colonel Lionel gives a gasp. He is trembling all over, for it chances that this brave soldier, who has led forlorn hopes in the Zulu war, and performed prodigies of valor on Egyptian battle-fields, has a peculiar dread of dogs, inherited from one of his parents.

It is not the animal that has fixed Lady Ruth's attention. Just in front and directly in the line of the dog's advance is a small native child that has been playing in the street.

He cannot be over three years of age, and with his curly black head and half-naked body presents a picture of robust health.

Apparently engrossed in his play, he sees and hears nothing of the clamor around until, chancing to look up, he sees the dog, and fearlessly extends his chubby arms toward it.

The picture is one never to be forgotten.

It thrills every one who looks on.

No one seems to have a gun or weapon of any kind. A peculiar paralysis affects them, a feeling of dumb horror.

A shriek sounds; from a window is seen the form of a native woman, who wrings her hands in terrible anguish.

The child's mother! God pity her! to be an eye-witness of her darling's fate!

Lady Ruth turns to the colonel, to the man who so recently proudly declared that no English woman ever asked a favor that a British officer would not grant, no matter what the risk.

"Save the darling!" her pallid lips utter.

He trembles all over, groans, takes a couple of tottering steps forward, and then leans against the wall for support.

"I cannot," he gasps.

Other Britons there are who would be equal to the emergency. Mortal man has never done aught in this world that Englishmen dare not imitate, and indeed they generally lead. It is unfortunate for England that an antipathy for dogs runs in the Blunt family.

This time Lady Ruth does not say "coward," but her face expresses the fine contempt she feels. With that mother's shrieks in her ears, what can she think of a man who will hesitate to save a sweet child, even at the risk of meeting the most terrible death known to the world?

St. George Rathborne

She turns to face the man who a short time before positively refused to risk his life because Miss Caprice desired it.

What can she hope from him?

As she thus turns she discovers that John Craig is no longer there, though three seconds before his hand was on her arm.

A shout comes from the street, where, when last she looked, not a living thing could be seen but the advancing mad dog and the kneeling child. A shout that proceeds from a strong pair of lungs, and is intended to turn the attention of the brute toward the person emitting it. A shout that causes hope to thrill in many hearts, to inspire a confidence that the innocent may be saved.

The young doctor from Chicago is seen bounding to meet the maddened brute, now so terribly close to the child.

None knows better than John Craig what the result of a bite may be. He has seen more than one hydrophobia patient meet death in the most dreadful manner known to the profession.

Yet he faces this fate now, the man who was thought too cowardly to crawl out along that bleak rock and secure a white flower for a girl's whim.

He goes not because it will be a great thing to do, or on account of the admiration which success will bring him. That mother's shriek of agony rings in his ears, and if he even knew that he was going to his death, yet would he still assume the risk.

It was on account of a mother—his own—he refused to risk his life before, and the same sacred affection inspires his action now, for he could never look into her dear eyes again, except in a shame-faced way, if he allowed this child to meet death while he stood an inactive spectator of the tragedy.

As he advances, John draws his right arm from his coat-sleeve. It is not the act of thoughtlessness, but has been done with a motive.

When the coat is free, with a quick motion he whirls it around, so that it rolls about his left arm.

Those who see the act comprehend his purpose, and realize that he means to force the brute to seize him there.

All this has occurred in a very brief time. Perhaps a quarter of a minute has elapsed since Lady Ruth turned to Colonel Lionel, and besought his aid.

John Craig has at least accomplished one purpose. Just as the mad dog is about to snap at the child, the young medical student snatches the boy away, and throws him to the rear. The child rolls over and over, and then, sitting up, begins to cry, more from surprise at the rough treatment than because he is hurt.

There is no time for John to turn and fly, and pick up the child on the way.

The dog is upon him.

John has only a chance to drop on his knee, and thrust his left arm forward.

Those who are watching, and they are many, hold their breath in dread suspense.

St. George Rathborne

"Heaven preserve him!" says Lady Ruth, wringing her clasped hands in an agony of fear.

They see the youth, he is hardly more, offer his bound arm to the beast, and those glittering fangs at once close upon it.

Then, quick as a flash, having filled the dog's jaws, John Craig throws himself forward, his whole effort being to crush the animal to the ground by his weight.

It is the work of a strategist. A veteran hunter when met by a fierce panther could not do better than this.

As John has expected, the dog, taken by surprise, does not offer the resistance that his powerful strength would warrant, but is at once borne backward, nor can he release his hold from the cloth-bound arm which his teeth have seized upon.

A struggle under such circumstances must be a terrible thing, and the shorter it can be made the better.

They see the man throw himself upon the brute; they know his other hand has sought the animal's throat, as the only means of ending his existence.

Prayers for his safety arise from many a heart, as the people watch the dreadful conflict from windows, and balconies, and other places where they have sought refuge.

The struggle is of brief duration.

John has the advantage in the contest, and the desire in his soul to prevent this mad beast from injuring others lends him a strength beyond what is naturally his portion.

With a grip of iron he clutches the brute's throat, and in a few moments the dog stiffens in death.

The young medical student arises, but the ferocious brute lies there harmless in the roadway. The smallest child in Valetta may play on the street now and fear no evil, thanks to the love one American bears for his mother.

Now that the danger is past, people flock out.

With the rest our tourists hasten toward the young hero. A form flies past them with wild eyes and disheveled hair; a form that pounces upon the little chap still crying in fright, and presses him convulsively to her breast.

That is the mother of the child.

They rush to the spot, some to congratulate the youth who slew the dog, others to gaze upon the horrible spectacle the animal presents as he lies there devoid of life.

Lady Ruth comes with the rest, and upon her fair face and in her sunny eyes can be seen a warmth of keenest admiration, such as poor Blunt failed to receive when he leaned far over the dizzy precipice to secure the flower Miss Caprice desired.

"Oh, doctor, how noble of you! I shall never forgive myself for the foolish blunder I made. See! these people look upon you as a hero, for you risked your life for a child of Malta. I am proud to be known as your friend."

Her looks as well as her words are enough to send any man into the seventh heaven of delight.

John Craig is very white; a set look is upon his face, but he smiles a little.

"I am glad the little fellow was not touched."

"And you?" she gasps, a sudden fear arising.

He slowly unwinds the coat which was thrust into the mad dog's mouth, and then rolls up his shirt-sleeve, to disclose to her horrified eyes the blue imprint of two fangs in the muscular part of his forearm.

CHAPTER III

SAVED BY FIRE

She looks up into his eyes; there is a set expression to be seen there, but his face is no whiter than before, although it must be a terrible shock to any man to see the imprint of a mad dog's teeth in the flesh of his arm.

"Oh, it has happened, the worst that could come about! What will you do, doctor?"

He is a man of medicine, and he knows full well what such a wound means.

"There is only one thing to be done. Excuse me for a minute or two, Lady Ruth."

He springs away from her side, and, turning with surprise, she sees him dart into the smithy of a worker in iron, just down the road a bit.

"Let us follow him!" says Philander.

"Poor, poor boy!" remarks Aunt Gwen.

"Oh, aunt! do you believe he will go mad?" gasps the

St. George Rathborne

younger lady, in a trembling voice.

"I am afraid; I've known of cases that happened like this. One thing's in his favor."

"And that?"

"He wasn't bit in the face, or on the hand."

"How does that matter?" demands Sharpe.

She gives him a look of scorn.

Then, ignoring her spouse, she says, as if continuing her speech to Lady Ruth:

"The dog's teeth went through several thicknesses of woolen cloth before entering the skin. The fabric very probably absorbed the poison. A rattlesnake's fangs are a different thing; they cut through the cloth and the poison is then injected from the hollow teeth or fangs."

"Oh!"

They have reached the smithy, and, standing in the door-way, witness a singular scene.

The smith is a brawny native Maltese, with a form a Hercules might envy. He has just taken from the fire a slender rod of iron, one end of which is hissing hot, even red.

With this he advances upon John Craig, who has laid his arm, bared almost to the shoulder, upon a high window ledge.

Then the iron just touches the flesh, and a little gust of white smoke puffs up.

"Jove! the boy has grit," mutters Colonel Lionel, unable to restrain his admiration, even for a rival in love.

As if overcome with the sensation of inflicting such pain, the blacksmith shudders and draws back.

"Again, it is not near enough," cries John Craig.

The blacksmith shakes his head.

"I cannot," he says, in English.

"My life may depend on it, man. This is no time for hesitation. Give me the iron!"

His words are spoken with authority, and the brawny smith surrenders the rod of glowing iron.

Without an instant's hesitation, only compressing his lips firmly together, the Chicagoan presses the red-hot iron upon his arm.

Then he tosses the hissing thing aside, and begins to draw his shirt over the raw red scar an inch square, which the merciless brand has seared upon his white arm.

Seeing the blanched face of Lady Ruth, and the anxious countenances of the others near-by, the doctor, who has recovered from the shock, smiles in a reassuring way.

"I am sorry you saw this; I didn't intend you should. Let us go to the hotel!" he says, slipping a coin in the hand of the honest smith, who seems loth to accept it.

Then the party continue down in the direction of the hotel, where they stop while the steamer undergoes repairs.

"Colonel Blunt, will you do me the favor to come to my room? I want to put a small bandage with iodoform on the burn," he says aside, but Lady Ruth hears it.

"Colonel Blunt, indeed! What sort of trained nurse do you suppose he would make? I have had experience—you may smile if you like. Tell the colonel where to find your box of liniments and bandages, and bring it to me."

"But, my dear Lady—"

"Not a word, doctor. I shall esteem it an honor; and what I lack in scientific knowledge my aunt can supply."

This clinches the matter, and John can offer no further argument against her wish; so Blunt, the Royal Engineer officer, is sent after the doctor's case, which errand he performs willingly enough, for although he knows this affair has brightened up the chances of his rival, still, as an Englishman, he has a deep, inborn admiration for bravery, no matter whether shown in a Zulu warrior, armed with war club and assagai, or in a Yankee youth who throws himself between a dusky child of Malta and a mad dog, to receive the monster's attack.

So he hastens up stairs to the room which John Alexander Craig temporarily occupies, opens the door, and speedily returns with the little traveling case in which the young physician keeps many important medicines, an assortment of ready liniment and lint, with the wonderful remedial agents known to modern surgery.

To John's surprise, after he has opened the case and started to arrange the small bandage, it is gently taken from his hands.

"Allow me," says the pretty "doll," as he has at times been forced to mentally term Lady Ruth, after she has played with his admiration.

"But, do you know—"

"I never told you my uncle was a surgeon, Sir Archibald Gazzam—"

"What! that great man your uncle!" cries the student, with the deep respect a young M.D. has for a famous practitioner.

"Yes; and more than once I have assisted him in some simple case at the house. He gave me credit for a fair amount of nerve."

"Fair amount! Jove! for a girl you have a wonderful quantity. Why, I believe you'd have faced that brute yourself, if I hadn't gone," he says, enthusiastically, the others being momentarily at the window to witness a procession pass the hotel, with the dead dog on a litter.

"No, no, I could not do that; but, Doctor Chicago, was that what sent you out to meet that awful beast?"

Her head is bent over her work, so that the intense blush remains unseen, but it fades away at his cool reply.

"Oh, no; quite another thing! I told you I never considered myself a coward, and when I saw that dear little child apparently doomed to a terrible death, I could see the eyes of one I revere looking at me, and though death were sure I could not refrain."

St. George Rathborne

He says this quietly and earnestly, yet without an apparent desire to arouse any feelings of chagrin on her side.

Lady Ruth bites her lips, but her hands are steady, and the touch is exceedingly gentle as she binds up the ugly red mark which he has inflicted on himself with what she is disposed to term Spartan-like courage.

"There; it is done, doctor."

"And neatly done, too," says Aunt Gwen, with a nod and a look of pride.

"I thank you sincerely, Lady Ruth."

"Ah! you are a thousand times welcome. There is not a woman in Valetta who would not feel it an honor to bind up the wound of the hero who saved that Maltese child," says this young lady, frankly.

More shouts without.

This time the men of Valetta are clamoring for the American to show himself. They do not know much of America, but they recognize true grit wherever they meet it.

Of course, a rush is made for the balcony, but John remains behind.

He is feeling somewhat weak after the exciting events of the afternoon.

And, as he sits there, smiling to hear the clamor without—for he is human, this young Chicago M.D.—some one touches his arm.

"Lady Ruth, I thought you went out with the rest," he stammers, with a guilty blush, for it chances that at the very moment he is thinking of her, and what a soft, electric touch she has, so soothing, so very delightful.

"I did not go; I was watching you."

"An interesting study, surely."

"It was to me. I desired to know whether you secretly feared the results of your wound."

"And I did not dream you were so concerned about me. Considering the matter calmly, I am disposed to believe there is now no danger—that the hot iron radically destroyed the last chance of infection."

"I am very glad to hear you say so."

"You care a little, then?"

How quickly she is on her guard.

"Because I would not see a brave boy needlessly sacrificed."

"You look on me as a boy. I am twenty-three."

"My own age, sir. That gives me the right to feel myself your senior."

"How so?"

"You know a woman is older at twenty-three than a man. Then you do not wear a beard."

"I shall cultivate one from this hour. Why, a year ago I

looked like a pard, but was influenced to change."

Again that quick flash of intelligence.

"Ah! Doctor Chicago has left a lady love in the city on the lake."

"What makes you say that?"

"Several remarks you have made; the one just now, and then in reference to the spur that sent you to face that dog. Ah! my friend, it must have been a strong motive to influence you like that."

He overlooks the peculiar patronizing air, such as a young woman sometimes assumes toward a boy her junior.

"Lady Ruth, the person you refer to, the thought of whom sent me to save that child, bears what is to me the holiest name on earth—mother."

She draws a quick breath.

"Forgive me. I was rude."

"Not at all. My words admitted of just such a meaning as you placed upon them."

"You left her in Chicago, of course."

John looks at her steadily.

"Lady Ruth, it may sound strange to you after what I have said, but my memories of my mother are all confined to the far past, to a period when I was a mere child; but they are none the less previous on that account."

She looks puzzled, as well she may.

"Do you mean she is—dead?"

"Heaven forbid, but I have not seen her in all these years. That is one reason I am abroad, Lady Ruth. I have a sacred mission to perform—to find my mother—to seek the solution of a mystery which has embittered my life. Perhaps some time, if we know each other a little better, I may confide a strange and sad story to you."

"Just as you please, doctor," she replies, with deep feeling in her voice, and at this moment the others bustle in.

"You must show yourself on the balcony. The dear people clamor for a sight of you, and I am really afraid they'll tear the house down soon if you don't appear before them," says Aunt Gwen, with unusual vigor.

"Yes, they unquestionably desire to publicly show their appreciation of your services, and I for one feel proud to be an American this day."

"Philander!"

"Excuse me, my dear. John, my boy, allow me to lead you out."

"One minute, please," says Lady Ruth, who has made a comfortable sling of a long white silk kerchief, which she wore around her neck.

This she insists on securing over John's shoulder.

"That arm must be painful. I know it from my long experience as the reliable assistant of my surgeon uncle. You will be glad to have this."

"But—for such a mere scratch—people will laugh at me," he protests, feebly, though it may be noticed that he makes no effort to deliver himself from the silk sling which she is now tying.

"People laugh at you! A mere scratch! Confound it, boy, there isn't a man living who would go through with what you have to-day for a cool, hundred thousand. I know one man a million would not tempt," cries the professor.

"I suppose I must submit," and accompanied by Philander, with the two women bringing up the rear, he passes out upon the balcony, where the colonel of Royal Engineers has remained, to be a curious spectator of the scene.

At sight of the hero of the street drama, those in the square before the hotel shout and cheer. They are mostly natives, but men and women feel very strongly drawn toward this young, smooth-faced American who risked his life to save a child, and that child a Maltese boy.

John bows, and presses his uninjured hand upon his heart, bows again, and retires.

Slowly the crowd disperses.

Lady Ruth completely ignores the colonel, but that veteran is not crushed by any means. He watches the capricious maiden with a quizzical light in his eye, which shows that he has not yet lost confidence in the kindness of fate, or his own charms as a beau.

Lionel Blunt's success in life has come from the fact that he has ever been ready to watch his chance and take advantage of every possible opportunity.

So night settles over Malta, over the dreamy, blue Mediterranean, over the singular city of Valetta, where this little
company of tourists have been temporarily marooned, and
where Doctor Chicago, aided by fate, has been enabled to
make his first charge upon the heart of the proud English
girl, Lady Ruth.

St. George Rathborne

CHAPTER IV

A WORLD-WIDE SEARCH

It is a night of nights, destined to mark, as with a white stone, the progress of at least two life currents that have until recently flown contentedly on, each in its own individual channel.

Valetta, being a city of the Italian school, makes much ado over the coming of Lent. The people, as if to prepare for six weeks of fasting, indulge in all manner of feasting.

Even the Mohammedans, who are present in no small numbers, join the festivities, for they, too, have a period of fasting, according to the example set by the prophet, and commanded in the Koran.

Hence Valetta is very gay when night comes on; fancy Chinese lanterns hang in the streets, music is heard on every hand, and laughing, good-natured crowds jostle elbows in a way that would horrify a high caste Hindoo.

Valetta has long been known as the headquarters of the famous Order of Malta. The representative commanderies of different nations have their inns, each called an *auberge*, on the principal streets, while the palace of the Grand Master is three hundred feet on each side, facing four streets, with a large square in front known as the Piazza St. Giorgio.

A small tower on the top known as the *Torretta* is used as a station from which men-of-war are signaled.

Everywhere can be seen the insignia of this ancient order, the white Maltese cross on a blood-red field, arousing thoughts of men in armor, the crusades, and much that is stirring and romantic in the history of the centuries that are gone.

A student of history would find much to entrance him in this peculiar hill-side city on the British Island of Malta.

Supper is served at the hotel just as night comes on, and John Craig, M.D., has managed to eat in an unconcerned way, talking with his friends, and trying to appear unconscious of the fact that two score of curious eyes are upon him, the incident of the afternoon having spread like wild-fire among the rest of the delayed steamer's passengers who stop at the same hotel.

This is the first time the young master of medicine has found himself the center of observation, and he comes through the ordeal very fairly, as Lady Ruth informs him laughingly, when they *by chance* leave the dining-room together.

Another ordeal awaits John. In the parlor he finds the mother of the boy whose life he saved. She cannot talk much English and John is hardly at home in Arabic, or the mixed language used by the Maltese.

When two persons are very much in earnest they manage to get on, and the poor woman calls down the blessings of Heaven on his head ere she leaves.

"I wish all this were over," he laughs, rejoining the English girl.

"Make the most of it, doctor," says the colonel, sauntering up with a choice weed between his teeth; "such occasions come rarely and had better be appreciated. Take the advice of an old campaigner, and make hay while the sun shines."

"Oh! I mean to, colonel," replies John, and there is a hidden meaning in his words that causes the officer to look at him steadily and mutter:

"Hang the boy! I really believe he expects to enter the lists against me, Colonel Lionel Blunt, who carries a Victoria Cross and knew what a love affair was before he was born. Well, the end is not yet, and he laughs loudest who laughs last."

All of which is very true, and proves that the colonel of Royal Engineers does not mean to let the opportunity pass.

A few minutes later John and Lady Ruth stand on the piazza of the hotel. The scene is well worth looking at, with its many lights, bright colors, and constantly changing crowds.

She expresses surprise, and seeks an explanation which fortunately the young doctor is able to give, thanks to certain information he picked up in scanning his guide book.

"In time of peace prepare for war. They seek by a double allowance of gayety to make up for the amount to be lost during Lent," he says.

"Is Mr. Craig here?" asks a voice, and all look at the speaker, who is a quiet appearing man, perhaps a native of England.

"That is my name, sir."

"John Alexander Craig?"

"The same."

"Of Chicago?"

"Well, what can I do for you?"

The other has been looking at him steadily.

"I desire to speak a few words with you, Doctor John Craig."

"Go on."

"I beg your pardon—it must be in private."

"In that case my friends will excuse me for a few minutes."

"Oh! yes," replies Lady Ruth, looking at the bearer of the message again.

"Certainly," says Blunt, promptly dropping into the chair John vacates at her ladyship's side, and his celerity to take advantage of the circumstance arouses a little suspicion in her mind that after all it may be a ruse to get him away, with the Briton's gold backing it.

She pays little attention to what the colonel is talking about; twice she turns her head and looks to where John and the stranger talk, while to herself she says:

"Strange why I am interested in him and his fortunes. What is this singular story concerning his mother, which some time he means to tell me—when we become better friends?

And now comes this man to hold a secret consultation with him! Where have I seen him before, where heard his voice? I cannot remember just now, but there is something familiar about him. The doctor appears to be excited—there, he lays his well hand on the other's arm and speaks quickly. Pshaw! it's none of my business," and she resolutely turns her face toward the bright scene on the street, only to glance back again a dozen seconds later.

The doctor comes up; singularly enough Lady Ruth has just bethought herself of her fan, and the military figure of the stalwart Briton is seen passing through the door-way upon a wild-goose chase for the much maligned article of ladies' warfare, which has played its part in many a bit of diplomacy, and which he will never find, as it is at that moment resting in the folds of milady's dress, cleverly hidden from view.

"I trust you have had no bad news, doctor?" says the English girl, with a touch of sympathy in her voice.

"On the contrary, Lady Ruth, I have heard something that is of intense moment to me," he replies, showing emotion.

"About—your mother?" she asks, quickly.

"It is so. Lady Ruth, you have heard me speak enough of my past to realize that it has been a lonely life. My father loves me after his own fashion, and I—respect him deeply; but all my life I have longed for the love of a mother, until it has reached an intensity you can hardly comprehend. Now I have received certain news that gives me a wild hope."

"I, too, lost my mother when young, and that circumstance enables me to feel for you."

Her tender eyes thrill him as he never yet has been touched; the bond of sympathy is akin to love; he has never had a confidant, and human nature yearns to unbosom itself.

"I promised to tell you the story, Lady Ruth. If I were sure we would not be interrupted, I would be inclined to speak now, for I am about starting upon a mission, the result of which Heaven alone can foresee."

His earnestness impresses her ladyship; trust a bright girl for bridging over a trifling difficulty such as this.

"There is a little private parlor attached and generally empty," she suggests, artlessly.

"Just the ticket," he boldly exclaims.

In a few minutes they are seated alone in this bijou parlor; its decorations are quaint, even barbaric in their splendor, and a lover of the *bizarre* would happen upon such a scene with the keenest of pleasure.

"Here are some drawings we can be looking over," she suggests, and he nods eagerly, inwardly blessing her ready sagacity.

Thus they look harmless enough.

"Now I will play the lady confessor. What is it all about? Have you fallen into debt like a bad boy, and don't dare write the *pater*?"

He looks at her and laughs.

"You see the comical side of everything, Lady Ruth. This I fear bids fair to be a tragedy."

"A tragedy! Dear me, didn't we have quite enough of that this afternoon? What can it be? Surely, you and the colonel—" and she colors furiously upon realizing how near she has come to betraying her thoughts.

"The colonel and I have had no words, as yet, Lady Ruth. This affair is something that concerns my past. Let me briefly tell you a few facts that are of especial interest to me, and may claim your attention.

"I told you I had not seen my mother since I was a child, yet she is not dead. An unfortunate affair happened, and she was exiled from home. Heaven knows I have ever believed her innocent.

"On several occasions, unbeknown to my stern father, I have received a line without a signature, a line that called down Heaven's blessings on my head, a line that caused me to cry like a baby.

"Thus year by year my resolve became stronger; I would find my mother, I would seek the solution of the dreadful mystery that hangs over the Craig home.

"My studies were done; I graduated at the head of the medical class and spent a year under the most eminent professors at Heidelberg. When they gave me my diploma, they wrote my father that I ought to have a year of travel to improve my health before entering upon the life work to which I am devoted.

"Of course my desire was granted, and I began the search. I have been six months at it without success; it is like pursuing an *ignis fatuus*. A clew would take me to Russia, whence I would fly to Persia, then to Turkey, and next to London. In Paris I felt sure of success, but the lady I was tracking turned out to be a grandmother, and there was a lively scene in her house when I sprung my game.

"Talk of 'Japhet in search of his father!' why, he wasn't in it at all compared with me. At last came another clew; among the letters forwarded in a bunch from home was a line in the same precious hand. See, here it is."

He takes out from a note-book a slip of paper; the writing is elegant and feminine.

She reads:

"January 12th. Just twenty years to-day. Oh! Heaven! teach me to kiss the rod."

No signature, only a mark like a tear-drop.

"Now you realize my position; you can, in a measure, understand the peculiar mingling of love, reverence, and pity with which I think of this mother, and how the thought of her enters into every act of mine."

"Yes, yes, I do indeed," sympathetically.

"I have sworn to find her—to let her know there is one who loves the poor exile. Let my father rage if he will, my heart burns to meet her. I will proceed. This letter was postmarked Malta, here at Valetta."

"But you did not mention—"

"I knew the steamer would stop a few hours at least, and thought that might be enough in which to learn the truth. Strange things have happened since we landed. I have learned several facts which astound me.

"You saw a man come in and draw me aside? That man controls the destinies of these people of Valetta, even as a chief of police would in our cities. When first I landed I sought the presence of Luther Keene—"

"There—your mention of his name revives my recollection like a flash. Now I know just when and where I met that man," she says.

"He promised to assist me, for a consideration, of course, and was especially delighted at the chance to prove that even out here in Malta there might be a second Vidocq.

"In his first report he told me the party I sought had been in Valetta only recently, but he believed she was now gone.

"The man told me just now where Blanche Austin staid during her residence here, at a house on the Strada Mezzodi, and I shall go as soon as I leave you, to make inquiries there. If you are interested in my story, you might, perhaps, care to hear what news I may pick up on my visit to this house, which has so recently covered my mother."

"Indeed, I am more than interested in your story, and anxious to learn how you succeed. Would you know your mother if you should meet her to-day?" she asks, mentally wondering why he has taken her into his confidence.

"I believe so. A son's loving eyes would do much toward solving the problem."

"But your memory of her must be exceedingly hazy, to say the least."

"That is true; but I have another clew. Once, when a boy, I was rummaging through some old papers in an antique secretary which I found in the attic, when I ran across an ivory miniature that had been overlooked.

"Upon it was painted a girl's face; my heart told me who it was, and underneath I found the words 'Blanche Austin at eighteen.'"

"I have treasured that ever since; it has been my most valued possession. Would you like to see it, Lady Ruth?"

"Must assuredly," she replies, warmly, eagerly.

He places it in her hands.

"It was plain when I found it; with my spending money for a whole year I had that gold locket made which holds it now. Ever since it has been very close to my heart."

"Such devotion is wonderful. I sincerely hope it will meet its reward."

Then she looks at the miniature, which time has not in the least harmed, looks at it—and utters a little ejaculation.

"She was beautiful indeed, Doctor Chicago—most charming. A face to haunt one. I can see a trace of sadness in it, even at this early age, as though her coming troubles cast a shadow before. You will be surprised when I tell you I have met her."

CHAPTER V

THE PROFESSOR ACTS

The medical student looks at her eagerly.

"When—where?" he asks, huskily.

Any one who has met the woman about whom cluster all the tender associations and thoughts of his lonely years of childhood, must assume new importance in his eyes.

"It was a year or so ago. At the time I was in Paris with my uncle, Sir Hugh, then alive."

"Yes, yes, she was there about that time, as I have since learned."

"I was out driving alone; it was just at dusk when we were returning from the boulevards, and a wheel came off the vehicle.

"Though a little alarmed, I kept my senses, and bade the driver tie his horse and then seek another vehicle for me.

"The neighborhood chanced to be a rather unsavory one. I could hear boisterous men singing, and on finding myself alone I grew alarmed. From windows frowzy heads were thrust out and rude women mocked at me. I feared insult, injury. I was ready to fly for my life when a hand touched my arm, and a gentle voice said:

"Come with me, miss, I will protect you."

John trembles with emotion.

"Then you have heard her speak! Oh, what bliss that would be for me—my mother, my poor mother who has suffered so long."

"When I looked in her face I knew I could trust her. Besides, her garb reassured me."

"Her garb?" wonderingly.

"Yes. She was dressed as a Sister of Charity or some other order in Paris. Willingly I followed her to an adjoining house. She begged me to sit down and await the vehicle. I was grateful and asked her questions about the great work being done by such organizations in the gay city of Paris.

"I was interested in her and asked her name. She told me she was known as Sister Magdalen. Then the carriage came and I left her."

"One question, Lady Ruth—how did she impress you?"

"Frankly, as one who had passed through the furnace of affliction; her face was sad, yet oh, so inexpressibly sweet. It haunted me. I have looked at every sister I met wherever I traveled, in the hope of meeting her, but it has been useless."

It can be readily believed that this arouses the deepest

interest in the young student of medicine. The desire to find his mother has been the one aim of his life; it has carried him over many a dark crisis, and has become stronger with the passage of years.

Now he is getting daily, hourly, nearer the object of his solicitude, and his anticipation so long and fondly cherished, bids fair to be a realization.

"How I envy you, Lady Ruth. You have seen her, pressed her hand. It makes you seem less a stranger to me to think that my mother was able to do you a service."

"I am positive it was she. Wait—perhaps I can prove it. I noticed she had a medallion secured around her neck with a guard, and once I was enabled to see the face upon it. It was that of a man."

"Oh! describe it if you can."

"The gentleman, I should judge, was about twenty-three. He wore a mustache and small side whiskers. I judged he was English. His hair was light and inclined to be curly."

John Craig smiles.

"Ah! the last doubt has been swept away."

"You recognize this picture, then?"

"Yes; your description answers for my father when he was a young man. I have not the slightest doubt that it was the one I seek who rendered you this service. And she a Sister of Charity! I don't understand."

"Your story has interested me deeply, doctor. You have my

most sincere wishes for success; and if I can in any way assist you, don't hesitate to call upon me."

"I believe you mean every word of it, and from my heart I thank you. I must leave you now, to seek the house in the Strada Mezzodi—the house that may reveal much or little."

At this moment the others enter; fortune has been kind to allow the conversation to reach its legitimate end, and John, with a pleasant word for Aunt Gwen and her husband, and only a peculiar look for the Briton, hurries out.

In five minutes more he comes down stairs, ready for the street. To his surprise he is stopped near the door by some one he knows—Philander Sharpe, wearing a ridiculous helmet hat, as becomes a traveler.

"Pardon me, but I'm in a hurry," he says, as the other plucks his sleeve.

"Oh! yes; but I'm going with you, Chicago," pipes the little professor, shutting one eye and nodding in a very knowing manner.

"But I'm not off to paint the town red," says John, believing the other thinks it is his intention to see the sights of Malta's capital by night—"I have an engagement."

"In the Strada Mezzodi; eh?"

"Thunder; how did you guess it?" ejaculates the man of medicine, astonished beyond measure.

"I am not a guesser. I know what I know, and a dused sight more than some people think, especially my beloved wife, Gwendolin."

"What do you know—come to the point?"

"First, all about your past, and the trouble in the Craig family."

"Confusion! and you never told me you had ever heard of me before? This explains the manner in which you seemed to study me at times on the steamer," reproachfully.

"Just so. I had reasons for my silence; *she* was one of them," jerking his thumb over his shoulder in the direction of the parlor above, whence the voice of the amiable Gwendolin Makepeace floats to their ears.

"In haste, then, let me tell you a secret, John. I was not always what you see me, a docile, hen-pecked man. Twenty-five years ago Philander Sharpe, young, good-looking, conceited, and rich, had the world before him."

"Cut it short, I beg, professor," groans John, impatient to be off.

"I fell in love; my affection was returned; we were engaged; a friend in whose honor I fully believed stole her heart away from me, but all these years I have never forgotten—never. John Craig, the girl I loved and who was to have been my wife was—your mother."

The little man folds his arms and throws his head back in a peculiar way he has. How strangely full of dignity these undersized people can be at times.

"Is it possible, and you never breathed a word of all this to me before?"

"Ah! my dear boy, the time was not ripe. I said nothing but

sawed wood."

"Why do you speak now?"

"I have an idea that you are about to make a step in the dark, and after duly considering the matter, came to the conclusion that it was time to speak—time to let you know my sympathies were with you, time to take a hand in this game myself."

John hardly knows what to do or say, he is so amazed at such a strange happening.

"But, professor, I am only going now to see if I can learn anything about my mother at the house where she staid six weeks ago, when a line was sent to me."

The little man wags his head wisely.

"That information was given to you by one whom you believed to be Signor Stucco, otherwise Luther Keene, the person having charge of the police of Valetta?"

"Yes," replies John, wonderingly.

"At that hour the signer was in his own room, engaged in other business, and oblivious of the fact whether one John Alexander Craig, M.D., was in the land of the living or not."

All of which excites the curiosity of the young man not a little.

"Since you know so much, professor, perhaps you can tell me who it is plays with me, the object he has, and whether my mother was ever in that house on the Strada Mezzodi."

"I can answer in part. I believe she was there. These enemies of yours, dear boy, have baited a trap. You are about to walk into it."

"A trap, professor! why should they seek to harm me?"

"They have reasons. I can't mention them all, but perhaps some event in your past may give you a clew. Have you ever heard of a person, by name Pauline Potter?"

The young man starts.

"Ah! I see you have," pursues Philander, dryly.

"I confess it; she was a pretty actress, but my boyish passion for her died out when I discovered her perfidy."

"Very true; but she has never forgiven you. What harm did you do her, boy?"

"The harm was on her side. When I found what deception she had put upon me I simply denounced her in the presence of several who were at supper with her, a new admirer among them. Perhaps she hates me for that, but it seems queer that Pauline Potter, whom I knew in Chicago, should bob up in Malta. Almost like a modern play."

"Well, she's here. I've seen her."

"Professor, pardon me for saying it, but you've allowed yourself to be maligned. I believed you were a nonentity, but I find you possessed of a remarkable mind. You are a second Richelieu."

"You flatter me. John, grant my favor; allow me to accompany you on this errand. I will then have a chance to explain how I managed to learn all these things."

"I see no reason to refuse."

"Good! Come, let's move off," with a quick glance over his shoulder.

"Oh," laughs the student, "*she's* up stairs yet," and his words are corroborated, for a burst of almost masculine laughter comes floating down from the next floor, causing Philander to shrug his shoulders.

"She'll imagine I'm off seeing the sights. I went to see the modern Mabille in Paris and have never heard the last of it. Stand by me in case of war, my boy."

"That I will, professor."

They have left the hotel, and John's face tells of the puzzle which he is trying to solve—the strange connection between Pauline Potter, the actress who won his boyish admiration only to deceive him, and she whom he seeks with reverent love in his heart, his mother, the Sister Magdalen of Lady Ruth's Paris adventure.

And the professor guesses the truth.

"I may be able to assist you, John, though you shall be the judge. Will you listen to my yarn?"

"With pleasure."

They walk on, arm in arm; the doctor has lighted a cigar, and seems to take much comfort in the mechanical puffs of smoke which he sends out into the darkness—not that there is anything of the inky pall about this, throwing a silvery path way along the mysterious waters of the romantic sea, and besides, the lanterns that flash on trees and from house fronts serve to render the scene far from gloomy, though a modern city dweller, used to electric lights, might notice the change.

"Before we enter into a discussion, my dear boy, let me explain how I came to know these facts connected with the presence of Pauline Potter in Valetta, and the duplicity of the man representing the head of the police, Signor Stucco.

"After returning from our eventful walk to the hill-top back of the town, I had business in another section, business connected with my trip along the Mediterranean, and which has been kept a secret from my spouse.

"When on my way back to the hotel, just at dusk, I crossed and passed down a street, thinking to shorten my route, but in a way became confused, and made up my mind I would inquire of the first person I came to.

"That, my boy, was the hand of fate leading me on, as you will speedily learn.

"In all these years that have flown I have at times heard of you. I knew the skeleton that lay hidden in your family closet, and believing your mother innocent, made no sign, for she was supposed to be dead.

"Let me go back a step, and begging your pardon for the fact, confess that I heard your interesting interview with Lady Ruth."

"Professor!" in reproach.

"My dear boy, it was all an accident. I had thrown myself

upon the lounge in the corner of the little parlor, for an after-dinner nap, when you came in and failed to notice me, owing to the arm-chair I had drawn in front of me to shut out the light.

"At first I thought you would simply look at the picture and then go away, but when I heard you telling her your sad story and the new hopes you entertained, I felt that I had a right to listen then. Thus you understand how I know these facts.

"This takes me back to where I was lost in the streets of Valetta and forced to inquire my way. As luck would have it I saw a man before me, but ere I reached him he was joined by a woman.

"I stood still; in the dusk I heard him say something that gave me a thrill, and as near as I can remember those words were:

"'For love of you, Pauline Potter, I have assumed this disguise and become for the present Signor Stucco, the master of Valetta's police. Now give me orders; tell me how I am to win your favor; how bring to the Strada Mezzodi—' I heard no more, as his voice fell, but presently my ears, sharpened to an intensity, caught a name—it was—'Doctor Chicago.'"

"You interest me, professor; please proceed."

"Ah! that is all. I lost track of them and managed to work my way to the hotel in time for dinner. When that man called you out, I recognized the dim figure I had seen talking with the soft-voiced woman at dusk. It takes time for me to figure things out, and I must be beyond the range of her voice. That was one reason I lay down in the little parlor. When I heard you announce your intention of visiting the Strada Mezzodi I made up my mind to act quickly. That is why I tapped you on the arm, why I am now tramping at your side. Now let us

St. George Rathborne

probe deeper.

"Mark the first point; this Pauline is a shrewd creature, and doubtless possessed of more than an ordinary Corsican nature to hate so bitterly."

"Ah! you know her mother was a Corsican?"

"I believe I have heard it told in New York, and it is easy to realize the fact now. Pauline is a good hater—her father was Scotch I presume.

"What I want to point out is this—she has been investigating your record—the skeleton in your closet, or rather your family, is no secret with her."

"I understand that, sir. It is no accident, her presence in the same house my mother occupied."

"Well, as to that, you're not sure. That fellow who brought the news was paid to represent the head of the Valetta police, for they knew you had invoked official aid, and just as like as not he gave you an address that your mother never heard of."

"Well, here we are!" suddenly.

"Eh? This is the Strada Mezzodi?"

"Any objections to it?" laughing.

"Oh, no! one place is as good as another to me, in this Maltese city, where you seem to be climbing to paradise or descending into hades all the time. Only I'm glad I came."

"Why, professor?"

"Well," with a look down the street, "I'm afraid you'll need the services of a friend before long—that you are about to experience a sensation you won't soon forget," replies Philander, coolly.

St. George Rathborne

CHAPTER VI

PAULINE POTTER'S HOUR COMES

"It is possible!" declares John; "and under such circums-tances I shall indeed be glad to have a friend in need. At the same time it seems as strange to me to think Pauline Potter can be here—that the Chicago actress whom I once adored and with a youth's ardor swore to make my wife, can be here and bothering her head about one John Craig, M.D."

"It will soon be known. You have a good description of this house which the man supposed to be Luther Keene brought?" asks Philander, showing unexpected business qualities; indeed, he is proving more of a wonder to the young Chicagoan every hour.

"Yes, and can find it easily enough by the red lamp in front," he replies.

"I see such a light along the strado."

"That is, in all probability, our destination."

They advance, and in another minute are at the door of the domicile marked so conspicuously with a red light.

John allows himself a brief period of ecstasy as he remembers that his mother crossed this threshold only recently, and in his eyes this renders it holy.

Then he recovers his common sense, and is once more the wide-awake, vigilant John Craig who met the advance of the mad dog so coolly upon the hill road of Valetta.

"There's a knocker," says the professor.

"I'll try it," John replies, and as he swings the weight a ponderous sound ensues, a hollow clamor that is loud enough to arouse the whole street, John thinks.

"Great guns!" mutters Philander, "it's a great piece of luck there's no grave-yard near."

"How's that?" demands his companion.

"Well, that clang would arouse the dead," is the amazing reply.

Further conversation is cut short by the sound of footsteps within—a bolt is withdrawn, proving that the inmates of the house on the Strada Mezzodi do not have the Maltese sense of honor that makes the presence of locks and bars unnecessary.

Then the door is opened.

The red lantern gives a light that shows them the interior of this Valetta house, and in the brilliant illumination stands a man, a native Maltese servant.

John has arranged his plan of action in such an event. He hopes the man who opens the door may talk English.

"Good evening," he says, courteously.

The man returns the salutation gravely.

"I would see the gentleman of the house on business of importance."

"Are you Doctor Craig?"

"That is my name."

"John Alexander Craig?"

"The same."

"Of Chicago?"

"You hit it, my friend of Malta."

"Ah! you are expected—enter," is the surprising reply, and the professor calls his attention to it by a sly dig in the ribs.

They start to enter, when the faithful servitor of the house bars the way of the professor.

"Pardon; I said Doctor Craig."

"Well?" demands Philander, bristling up.

"You can wait for him outside. I will give you a chair, a cigar."

The professor laughs in good humor.

"Bless you, I'm Doctor Craig's shadow; he can't go anywhere but with me. Fetch two chairs. We will interview your master outside."

The citizen of Malta appears perplexed. John comes to the rescue.

"It will be all right; this gentleman is my companion, my interpreter. It is necessary that he accompany me. Enter, professor."

His assurance carries the day; the man backs down and allows Philander a passage.

Their first point is gained.

The servant having closed and barred the door and asked them to follow, goes on ahead. The professor takes advantage of the opportunity presented, and plucks John's sleeve, and as that worthy bends down, he whispers:

"Have you noticed it?"

"What?" asks the young doctor.

"His style of address, my boy; same words exactly that were used at the hotel by the man who brought you the news."

"Jove! you are right, professor. I imagine that must be the formal style in this country."

Philander chuckles.

"You'll have to guess closer to the mark than that, my boy, when you want to strike the truth."

"What can you mean, sir?"

"Bless you, it's the same man. Notice his walk; doesn't he hold himself just so?"

"Professor, you're wide awake. I admit all you say. There is a wonderful resemblance. Yes, I believe it is the same man. Really, this affair grows more and more interesting. Talk about your comedies, they're not in it."

Further conversation is cut off by the fact of their guide ushering them into a room that is lighted with an antique lamp.

"Wait here," he says, and disappears.

John Craig manages to retain his self-possession, though it gives him a thrill to think that he may be looking upon a scene which was only recently graced by the presence of the being whom he seeks far and wide—his mother.

Now some one comes; they hear the rustle of skirts, and know it is no man who advances.

"Steady, boy," warns Philander, knowing the sensation produced in John's quivering, expectant heart; "steady it is now, and keep your wits bright."

"Steady it is," replies John, who knows it is only right he should brace up.

Then the party advancing enters the apartment, and looking up the two men behold one who is garbed in a peculiar habit, the insignia of an order; a heavy black gown, corded at the waist, with a white flowing collar, and a strange bonnet both black and white, the size of which is astonishing.

Her face they do not see, as a gauze vail hides it from

mortal view.

In this city of orders, where the nations of the world seem to vie with each other in creating strange commanderies, it is nothing to meet with such a garb.

John Craig is a gentleman; he rises from his chair and bows; ditto Philander, who keeps a little in his rear, as becomes a sensible, well-behaved "shadow."

The dress of the woman gives John an idea she is at the head of some charitable organization which has set rules for dress and duty, although his knowledge of such matters is not most profound.

"Madame, pardon this intrusion," he says, at the same time wondering whether she is English, French, or a native of Malta.

Her reply comes in a low voice, and tells him she is as familiar with the English language as himself, no matter what her nationality.

"It is no intrusion, Doctor Craig. I have been expecting you."

"Indeed; you surprise me, madame, since I sent no word of my coming."

"Ah! a little bird sent me the news."

"Do you know why I enter your abode without an invitation, madame?"

"You seek news, Doctor Craig."

"That is true."

"News of one who has long been lost; news concerning a member of our holy order; the dear sister who has cones-crated her life to charity, and who, under my fostering care, has long since redeemed her past—Sister Magdalen."

The words almost unnerve John; he has a feeling that perhaps Heaven means to be kind and allow him the bliss he craves.

"Ah! madame, you know my secret. It is true. I would find her, would hear from her own lips the story of the past. I believe you can help me. She has occupied this house."

"That very chair upon which you are seated sustained her fainting form one afternoon when she came in. I thought she was dying. In her hand she carried a paper, an American daily. I glanced at it to see if I could learn the truth, and saw it there as plain as day. She had read a notice of a fire in Chicago where a young man named John Craig, said to be a medical student, perished."

"Did she see that account? It was cruel. The next day's paper refuted the lie, and explained how he escaped," says John, warmly.

"Yes, I saw it. She would give us no rest until we procured a later copy of the same paper, and there she read the truth. Sister Magdalen was all smiles from that hour; she said that Heaven had indeed answered her prayer."

"Tell me, is she here now?" holding his breath with suspense.

"Oh! no, she went away several weeks ago. We shall not see her again unless she chances to be one of three lay delegates now on their way here from a sister sanctuary."

"Then you can give me hope; let me know where I may find her?"

"If I see my duty in that way, Doctor Craig," is the astonishing reply he receives.

He conceives the idea what this may mean.

"Madame, I am ready to do what I can for the good of your order if you will bring about this long anticipated meeting."

"Your word shall be your bond. We need five hundred dollars to endow another bed in the hospital at Rome."

"It shall be yours; I swear it."

"Hush, impious man! Your word is enough. On my part I promise that ere an hour goes by you shall be in a fair way to look upon the face of one who loves you more dearly than if you had never been lost to her."

John hears and believes; he is not suspicious enough to put a double meaning upon the words.

"An hour—so soon? What am I to do in order to gain this consummation of my hopes?" he asks, in deep surprise.

"Nothing, only be content to remain here as my guests."

John looks at Philander and the latter nods, for it all seems clear and above board.

"We agree, madame," says the young doctor.

The Mother Superior, as they take her to be, bows her head solemnly.

"It is well," she says, and touches a bell.

Almost immediately the native servant appears, to whom she speaks in low tones, while John wonders when so great a revolution in the affairs of orders like this occurred whereby they are enabled to have men-servants.

Hardly has the native vanished than another sister appears, carrying a small tray upon which are seen a crystal bottle full of grape juice, three odd glasses and a plate of plain flat cakes.

"Doctor Craig, our order refuses the use of wines; this is the pure juice of the grape, expressed at our own vineyard on this island. It is as harmless as water, but refreshing. It is our simple habit to invite our guests to join us in this way; we believe in the Arab rule of breaking bread; those with whom we take salt are ever more our friends. You will not, cannot refuse."

How should they?

John looks at the professor, and in turn the latter looks at John.

"Madame, you have given me cause for happiness; we will join you in your simple lunch," returns the young man.

"You are wounded," noticing his arm in its sling.

"Not seriously."

"By chance I saw your adventure this day. I am proud to have the hero of that noble deed for my guest."

"Pardon; please do not mention it."

He accepts a glass of the grape juice and an anise-seed cake, for this plant is grown in Malta for export.

The liquid is cold and very refreshing. John has a dozen questions on the tip of his tongue, all of which relate to Sister Magdalen, but he does not put them, for his thoughts become somewhat incoherent, and it is so comfortable sitting there.

When the Mother Superior raises her vail to sip from the amber glass of unfermented wine John Craig, M.D., has sense enough to notice two things; the hand that holds the glass is plump and fair, and the lips under the vail form a Cupid's bow such as age can never know.

This arouses a wild curiosity in his mind; he wonders what this woman, who wears such a strange habit, can be like, and watches her with something of eagerness.

Surely the room is growing very close; a window opened would be a good thing he believes, and yet somehow lacks the energy to open it, turns his head, and sees the professor lying back in his chair *fast asleep.*

This gives him a faint shock, but his nerves are deadened; nothing would surprise him very much now, unless an earthquake occurred.

"Rest your head, Doctor Craig; the back of the chair is very comfortable," he hears a soft voice say.

Warm breath fans his face. The Mother Superior has thrown aside that ugly bonnet; it is a young, face, a fair face, surrounded by golden curls, that looks down upon him, as with a stage laugh the woman rests one hand on the head of the drugged medical student from Chicago, to exclaim:

"At last! he belongs to Pauline Potter!"

CHAPTER VII

THE BEAUTIFUL TIGRESS

John Craig dreams. He fancies himself bathing with demon apes in the wilds of Africa, having read an explorer's account of such a scene very recently.

They press him hard, and he can see no hope of escaping with his life.

In the midst of his mental torture he opens his eyes, and the disagreeable features of the case are suddenly swept away.

Where can he be? Soft music throbs upon the scented air, he hears the gentle plash of a fountain in a court near by; a mellow light, anything but garish, shows him the most luxurious surroundings, silks and velvets, brightness in color and gorgeousness in taste, everywhere.

This amazes him; almost takes his breath away; it is so different from his dream, which left him in a desperate hole.

His mind seems dull of comprehension, which must be the effect of the drug, so that for a brief time he is unable to understand the situation, or grasp his condition.

Then it dawns upon him, the mission that took him away from the hotel; and having reached that point, he is wrestling with what must have followed when something touches his face, something that is cool and pleasant—the soft, white hand of a woman.

Then Doctor Chicago's eyes flash open again, and he looks up startled; he has just recollected Lady Ruth's story, and a wild hope rushes into existence, a hope that could not be put into words, but which takes the form of an idea that she whom the English girl met as Sister Magdalen, his mother, is near.

He looks up; his eyes fall upon a face that boasts of extreme beauty, a face of wondrous black eyes and cheeks aflame, a face that, set in sable coils of hair, would drive an artist wild with the desire to transfer its charms to canvas.

And John Craig, strange man, frowns.

Evidently there is something in his composition that prevents him from accepting what the prodigal gods have thrown in his path.

"You?" he says, bluntly, and with disdain.

The woman with the black eyes smiles sweetly as she continues to soothingly touch his forehead, which throbs and burns as though he endures the keenest pain.

"Did you imagine it could be any other, my dear John? You deserted me, but I believe you failed to know your own mind. At any rate I have determined not to desert you."

"Pauline, you do not—it is impossible for you to care for me after what has happened."

"Impossible! Why should it be? I can't help myself. I have seen others profess to love me, have played with them as a queen might with her subjects who prostrated themselves before her. Yet, John Craig, I never loved but once. You have stirred my heart to its depths. I am not able to analyze these feelings. I only know what I know."

She does not feel the modesty of a young girl; much acting before the public has made her brazen, this midnight beauty with the glowing eyes black as sloes, the pouting lips, the figure of a Hebe.

John Craig may have seen adventures before in his life, and probably has been in many a fix, being fond of spending his vacations in rambling over the wilderness away up in the Michigan peninsula, with a gun on his shoulder; but plainly he has now met the crisis of his whole career.

"Pauline, I am a frank fellow, as you know. It is not in me to dissemble. I am going to speak plainly with you," he says, rising to a sitting posture, and looking the actress full in the eyes.

She moves uneasily, and her cheeks, which were erstwhile tinted with scarlet, grow pallid. Then she sets her teeth and with a smile continues:

"That is right, I hate a deceiver worse than anything else on earth. It was your honest way, John Craig, that first drew me toward you. Yes, speak your mind."

Evidently she is in part prepared for the worst, though she has hoped that the old witchery might be thrown about the young doctor.

"When you treated me in that merciless way, long ago, the

regard I felt for you died out of my heart—your spell was broken."

"Ah! John, you have thought so, perhaps, just as I did, but I learned that these affections of ours are deeper than we suspect. I believed I had dropped you forever, but time has taught me what a terrible wrench it must be that would tear the image of John Craig from my heart."

"I am sorry to hear you say so, Pauline, for on my part I have been effectually cured. I even look back and regard our love-making as a foolish, boyish fancy in which neither of us knew our own minds. Why can't you do the same?" he says, calmly.

"I am not built that way—my nature is of the tropical order, for my mother was born in Corsica, you know. Some of these fair English girls may be fickle, but Pauline Potter is the same as when she knew you in Chicago. But, John Craig, this same love can change to hate; it is but a step between the two, and no magician's wand is needed to make the transformation."

Already a change has swept over her face; it does not look so lovely now, for the arched black brows meet in a frown, while from the midnight eyes the fires of aroused passions begin to scintillate.

Craig knows that when he stirs up the pool he arouses the worst elements in her nature. Still he will not disguise his feelings and assume an ardor he is far from feeling.

Mentally he contrasts this girl with the English maid, and Pauline suffers by the comparison.

Perhaps a trifle of the scorn he feels shows upon his face.

Pauline can no longer call him her slave, and it may be this that arouses the new feeling in her heart, for a woman will never bear the sneers of one whom she has madly loved.

"This is worse than foolish, Pauline. You seem to know at least a portion of my mission abroad, and hence must be aware that I am in no humor for love-making—that my whole soul is bound up in my search."

"Well, I can help you, John," she says, quietly, holding her feelings in check until she has ventured upon this last resort.

"You can? Then I beg of you, Pauline, to give me assistance. To find my mother is the one thought of my existence, and any one who can shorten my quest must have my deepest gratitude."

Pauline frowns again.

"I hate that word; it has no place with me, John Craig. Friendship I despise—it is either love or hate with me. Let me tell you what I am in a position to do—find your mother for you, bring you face to face, or, on the other hand, render it impossible for you to ever set eyes upon her."

Her manner proves it to be no idle boast, but the young man will not descend to deceit, even when he might accomplish so much.

"Will you bring about this meeting?" he asks.

"On one condition, John."

"Well"—hesitatingly—"name it."

"That you marry me," is the prompt reply, and even Pauline,

actress by nature and vocation as she is, turns a trifle rosy under his gaze, though not abashed.

"That is a sudden ultimatum. Kindly tell me when you would like this little affair to come off?" he asks, lightly.

"Now—before I take you to the one you have long sought."

"Pardon me; I can hardly collect my wits. You see I had not dreamed of marrying for years. It is very, very sudden."

"Oh! I'll give you time to reflect upon it, John. I wouldn't hurry up such grave business."

"I don't believe I need much time. Don't you think it is a rather strange thing to demand payment before you deliver the goods?"

"If you gave me your word, John, I would wait until I had carried out my word."

"You think you could trust me?"

"I am willing to accept the chances."

"Indeed!"

"Will you make the promise?"

"Not I."

"Then you were simply gaining time," with a clenching of the small hands and a gathering of the black brows.

"I wanted to uncover your batteries; to learn what you knew; to understand your designs. Now that you give me no

St. George Rathborne

alternative, I am compelled to hurt your feelings by declaring myself able to find the one I seek without the aid of Pauline Potter."

As he speaks the last word he rises to his feet, once more feeling like himself.

"What would you do now, John Craig?"

"Leave this building, since I was lured here under false pretenses. What have you done with my companion?"

"The funny little man? Oh, he left here long ago when he learned you had fallen among old friends," she replies, carelessly.

John remembers something now; it is the sight of Philander Sharpe lying back in his chair drugged, and therefore he does not credit what the actress says.

"Will you show me the way out?" he asks.

"I will do more."

She claps her hands together in the oriental way of summoning a servant.

Instantly the curtains move; three men enter the apartment, and John realizes that Pauline Potter is about to show her teeth.

He draws his figure up, for while not a pugnacious man, he knows how to defend himself. As to his bravery who can question it after his action of the afternoon?

"Does it take three to show me to the door? With your

permission I will depart."

"Not yet Doctor Chicago—not yet."

"Ha! you would attempt violence. Well, I'm ready to meet these fellows, thanks to the forethought that caused me to arm myself before starting on this quixotic errand to-night."

The young Chicagoan throws a hand back, meaning to draw the little pocket revolver which has more than once served him well, but, to his dismay, it is gone.

He sees a derisive smile upon the features of Pauline, and knows she has taken it while he lay there unconscious on the couch.

"I was afraid you might do yourself damage, John. If you are wise you will submit tamely," she says, and clapping her hands again sets the three men upon him.

Craig is no Hercules in build, and besides, his left arm is in rather a poor condition for warfare, being exceedingly sore.

Still he is not the one to submit tamely so long as a single chance remains, and for the space of a minute there is a lively scene in the oriental apartment, in which divans are overturned, men swinging desperately around, and even Pauline Potter, accustomed to stage battles only, is constrained to utter a few little shrieks of alarm.

Then it is over.

Doctor Chicago, breathing hard and looking his dogged defiance, stands there in the hands of his captors.

"Do you change your mind, John Craig?" asks the woman,

fastening her burning gaze upon his face.

"I have too much Scotch blood in me for that. On the contrary, I am more than ever determined to pursue my mission without any outside assistance," he answers.

"Take him away!" she cries, and the look that crosses her face can only be likened to the black clouds preceding the hurricane.

John struggles no longer, for he realizes that he is safer out of her sight than in it.

They take him through a door-way and the last he hears from the beautiful tigress is her taunting cry of:

"We will break this proud spirit of yours, John Craig—what you scorn now you will beg for after awhile, when it is too late!"

He wonders whether this is a prophecy.

The men hurry him along a narrow hall, for many of these Maltese houses are built in a queer way, nor do they treat him with consideration, but rather the contrary.

When he ventures to protest, the man who opened the door orders silence and enforces it with a cowardly blow from his fist.

John looks him straight in the eye and says:

"You coward! I will remember that," at which the man turns his head away and swears under his breath.

Presently they halt in front of a door, which the leader

unlocks. At a word from him the young American is pushed inside.

John, receiving such an impetus, staggers and throws out his hands for support, but failing to find anything of this kind, pitches over, just as the door slams shut.

He recovers himself and sits up, a trifle bruised, but not otherwise injured through his rough treatment.

This is a nice predicament, to be shut up in a house of Valetta, while, perhaps, Philander Sharpe returns to the hotel with a story of his succumbing to the wiles of a beautiful enchantress.

The steamer will sail without him, and the duse must be to pay generally.

John begins, like a man, to wonder if he can do anything for himself; that spirit so distinctive, so Chicago like, will not allow him to sit down and repine.

Surrounded by gloom, how will he find out the nature of his prison?

He endeavors to penetrate the darkness—a trace of light finds an entrance under the door and relieves the somber blank. It does more, for all at once John's eyes discover something that rivets his attention.

There are two of them—eyes that gleam in the darkness like those of a great cat.

A thrill sweeps over the doctor; can it be possible they have shut him in here with some great fierce animal that will tear him limb from limb? Is this Pauline Potter's dramatic revenge?

St. George Rathborne

Who can blame him for a sudden quaking in the region of his heart—such a fate is too terrible to calmly contemplate; but this qualm is only momentary, and then Doctor Chicago is himself again, brave and self-reliant.

CHAPTER VIII

HER DEBT CANCELED

He begins to reason, to strain his mind in search of all the things he ever heard with relation to a meeting between unarmed men and wild beasts.

The power of the human eye has been held up as an example, and surely here is a chance to try it—the stake, his life.

By this time he becomes cognizant of a certain fact that renders him uneasy; the yellow orbs do not seem as far away as before, and it is evident that they approach gradually nearer.

He can even imagine the great body of the animal, perhaps a tiger from African shores, creeping on its belly, inch by inch shortening the distance between itself and its prey.

John cannot retreat—already he is in a corner, with the wall behind, so that all he can do is to await developments.

Nearer still, until scarcely five feet separate him from the glowing orbs, he can even hear the animal's stentorian breathing.

St. George Rathborne

John prepares for a terrible struggle; he holds his hands out so as to clutch the great beast by the throat as he advances, and his muscles are strained in order to sustain the shock.

Just when he expects to hear the roar of a hunger-stricken beast, he is astonished beyond measure at what occurs.

"Scat! you rascal!" exclaims a voice, and there is heard a great threshing sound, as though some one endeavors to intimidate by the swinging of arms as well as by sound.

"What! is that you, Professor Sharpe?" demands the doctor, amazed, delighted, not because he has a companion in misfortune, but on account of the dissipation of his fears respecting an assault.

In another minute the two are embracing; there is nothing like danger to bring men together and make them brothers.

There is strength in union, and both of them feel better since the meeting.

Of course their thoughts are wholly bent on escape, and the talk is of this. Sharpe has not been so thoroughly searched as his companion, and soon produces a few matches, with which they proceed to examine their dungeon.

It is a gloomy prospect.

The walls are heavy and of stone; there is no opening beyond a mere slit in the corner through which comes wafts of the sweet air without.

As to the door, it would withstand the assault of giants.

Hopeless indeed does it all appear, and yet little do we poor mortals know what the next minute may bring forth.

While they are seated there, seeking to cheer up each other, it is John's keen ears that detect the presence of some one at the door.

This is not a new event that may be pregnant with hope—on the contrary, it is possibly the next downward step in the line of Pauline Potter's revenge.

When the key turns in the lock, both men are on their feet ready to meet whatever may be in store for them.

The door swings open.

Instead of a man, they see a woman of Malta. Upon her arm hangs a lantern. She shades her eyes from its glare and looks upon the prisoners.

To say Doctor Chicago is surprised would be putting it feebly; he is amazed at the sight of a woman jailer.

Now she fastens her eyes on his face, he can almost feel her gaze. She advances a step or two.

"Chicago?" she says, inquiringly.

John hardly knows what she means.

"Answer her," says Sharpe, quickly; "she wants to know if you are from Chicago."

"Yes," returns Craig, nodding.

"Name?"

"John Craig, M.D."

"It is good. Come."

He is thrilled with a new hope. Can this mean escape? or does the clever Pauline play a new game with them?

"Shall we go, Sharpe?" he asks, in a whisper.

"Go—well, I reckon we'd be fools to let such a chance as this slip," returns the little man, instantly.

So they proceed to follow their strange guide, out of the dungeon door and along the narrow passage after her.

Again John suspects, and bends his head close to that of his comrade.

"Professor."

"Well, I'm wide awake. What is it you want?" returns the other.

"Do you really mean to trust her?"

"She seems friendly enough. We're out of that abominable place—bah! I'd as soon be shut up in the Calcutta Black Hole as there."

"But, Pauline—"

"Well, what of her?"

"She is a wonderfully shrewd girl, and this may only be one of her tricks."

"I don't believe it; she had us safe enough before. Besides, John, my dear boy, I seem to have discovered something that has not yet made itself apparent to you."

"Then tell me."

"You noticed how she stared at you and asked your name; why, it didn't matter if a dozen Philander Sharpe were near by."

"Yes, but get down to facts."

"She is repaying her debt."

"To me—she owes me nothing, man."

"You mistake. As you walk, doctor, don't you feel your left arm twinge some?"

"Hang it, yes; but what's that got to do with this Maltese woman with the lantern?"

"Softly—speak in whispers if you don't want to arouse the house. See, she turns and raises her forefinger warningly. Do you mean to say you don't remember her, John?"

"Her face is familiar, but—"

He hesitates, and faces the professor.

"I see, you've got it. You saved her child from the death fangs of the mad dog, and a kind Heaven has placed her in a position to return the favor, which she would do if the most terrible fate hung over her head."

"It seems incredible," mutters the doctor.

Nevertheless it is true; the one chance in ten thousand sometimes comes to pass.

Already has his afternoon's adventure borne fruit in more ways than one; first it restored him to his former place in the esteem of Lady Ruth, which his refusal to do her foolish errand had lost him, and now it works greater wonders, snatching him from the baleful power of the actress who, unable to rule, would ruin.

Truly he has no reason to regret that heart affection, that love for humanity which sent him out to snatch the dusky child of Malta from the fangs of the beast.

Now they have reached a door that is heavily barred, proving that their course has been different from the one by means of which they gained the dungeon.

The woman lays down her lantern and takes away the bars. Then she places her hand on John's arm.

"You saved my child, Chicago; I save you."

She smiles, this dusky daughter of Malta, as if greatly pleased at being able to frame her thoughts in English— smiles and nods at the young doctor.

"But you—she may punish you," he says, and she understands, shaking her head.

"She no dare; I am of Malta; also, I shall see her, this proud mistress, no more," which doubtless means that she intends taking French leave as soon as the Americans have gone.

John takes her hand and presses it to his lips; a dusky hand it is, but no cavalier of old ever kissed the slender member of a lady love with more reverence than he shows.

"Go, it is danger to stay," she says, with something of a look of alarm on her face, as from the interior of the dwelling comes some sort of clamor which may after all only turn out to be the barking of a dog confined in the court where the fountain plays, but which at any rate arouses her fears.

They are only too glad to do so; after being confined in that murky dungeon the outside air seems peculiarly sweet.

It must be very late, and in this quarter, at least, the noises of the earlier night have passed away.

The only sounds that come plainly to their ears are the booming of the heavy tide on the rocks, and the sweep of the night wind through the cypress trees.

When they turn again after making an effort to locate themselves, the door in the wall is closed, and the Maltese woman is gone.

There is no cause for them to linger, and they move away.

John Craig has nothing to say. The disappointment has been keen, and he does not yet see a ray of light ahead.

Hope had such a grasp upon his soul, when he started from the hotel, that the fall has been more disastrous.

Not so Philander Sharpe.

An evil fortune has kept him pretty quiet for quite a little while now, and he begins to make up for it in part, chirping away at a merry rate as they push their way along the street.

St. George Rathborne

At first Doctor Chicago pays little heed to what he says, but presently certain words catch his ear and tell him that the professor is not merely speaking for oratorical effect or to hear himself talk.

"What's that you say, sir?" he asks.

Cheerfully Philander goes back to repeat.

"I was saying that I experienced queer sensations when I came to. They had carried you away to some more luxurious apartment, but I was left where I went to sleep—anything was good enough for Philander Sharpe.

"At first I was dazed; the soft murmur of the fountain came near putting me to sleep again with its droning voice. Then I suddenly remembered something—a charming face with the flashing eye of a fiend.

"That aroused me to a comprehension of the position, and I no longer cared to sleep. Action was necessary. I knew they cared little about Philander Sharpe, as it was you the trap had been set for—hence I was perhaps in a position to accomplish something.

"I left my chair and prowled around. They had disarmed me, and my first natural desire was to find some sort of weapon with which I could do service in case of necessity.

"In thus searching I came across a peculiar knife, perhaps used as a paper-cutter, but of a serviceable kind, which I pocketed.

"More than this, I discovered something that I thought would prove of importance to you, and this I hid upon my person, very wisely, too, for a short time later I was suddenly set

upon by three miserable rogues, who crept upon me un-
awares, and in spite of my frantic and Spartan-like resistance, they bore me away along a dim passage, to finally
chuck me into the vile den where you came later and alarmed
me so dreadfully, as I fully believed it must be some tiger cat
they had been pleased to shut in with me."

The little professor rattles off these long sentences without
the least difficulty—words flow from his lips as readily as
the floods roll over Niagara.

When John sees a chance to break in he hastily asks what it
is the professor has discovered that interests him.

Whereupon Philander begins to feel in his various pockets,
and pull out what has been stored there. At last he utters an
exclamation of satisfaction.

"Eureka! here it is. Found it lying on a desk. Was attracted
by the singular writing."

"Singular writing! that makes me believe it must have come
from my mother."

"It is signed Sister Magdalen."

"Then that proves it; you remember what Lady Ruth said
about meeting a Sister in Paris who resembled the miniature
I have of my mother. It was a kind fate that brought this to
you, professor."

"Well, you see, I always had a faculty for prying around—
might have been a famous explorer of Egyptian tombs if I
hadn't been taken in and done for by Gwen Makepeace."

"Was there anything particularly interesting in this letter?"

asks John.

"I considered it so—you will see for yourself," is the reply.

All is darkness around them. John is possessed of patience to a reasonable extent, but he would like to see what this paper contains.

"Professor, you seem to have about everything; can you drum up a cigar and a match?"

"Both, luckily."

"Ah! thanks," accepting them eagerly.

"It may be dangerous to light up here," says Philander, cautiously, but the other is deaf to any advice of this sort.

There is a rustling of paper, then the match is struck, and Doctor Chicago is discovered bending low in order to keep it from the wind. His cigar is speedily lighted, and his eyes turned upon the paper which Philander has given him— Philander, who hovers over him now in eager distress, anxious to hear John's opinion, and yet fearful lest the rash act may bring danger upon them.

John's lips part to utter an exclamation of mingled amazement and delight, when from a point close to their shoulders an outcry proceeds; the burning match has betrayed them.

CHAPTER IX

BRAVO, PHILANDER!

It is impossible for them to understand just at the moment what has occurred.

They are in a part of the Maltese city that Europeans might well hesitate to visit at the hour of midnight, however much they would frequent it in daylight.

The natives of Valetta have not all become reconciled to British rule, and although no open outbreak occurs, more than once has it been placed in evidence that there is a deep feeling of resentful distrust in certain quarters, which only awaits an opportunity to show its ugly teeth.

Knowing this fact, it is general principles more than anything else that causes Philander to have concern.

When those loud cries break forth close at hand, he knows his fears were not without foundation.

John Craig is also suddenly brought to a realization of the fact that he has hardly been prudent in his action.

He stows the paper away with a single movement of his

St. George Rathborne

hand. It is precious to him, and must be kept for future study.

Then he is ready to face those who, by their presence and outcries, announce themselves as the foes of foreigners.

There are many secret societies on the famous island besides the Knights of Malta, and it is not at all improbable that an organization exists which has for its main object the eventual uprising of the Maltese and their freedom from the British yoke.

This would naturally be kept a secret, and not proclaimed from the flat roofs of Valetta, or the platform of St. Lazarus.

Philander has shown remarkable traits upon this night of nights, traits which Doctor Chicago never suspected he possessed. He now proves that, in addition to these other commendable qualities, he has wonderful presence of mind, and that no sudden emergency can stupefy his senses.

Just as soon as the outcry is heard, he draws the small, cimeter-shaped paper-knife, which he claimed would make a serviceable weapon.

At the same time he cries out:

"We're in for it, John, my boy! Don't be too proud to run. Legs, do your duty!"

With which remark Philander starts his lower extremities into action, turning his head to make sure that his companion has not hesitated to follow.

If the professor is a small man, he has the faculty for getting over ground at quite an astonishing rate of speed. His short legs fairly twinkle as they measure off the yards; and, given a fair show, he would lead any ordinary runner a race.

The darkness, the uneven street, and his unfamiliarity with his surroundings, are all against him now, so that he cannot do himself justice.

Suddenly he misses his companion. John was close beside him ten seconds before—John, who is a sprinter from athletic education, and who could have distanced the professor with only half an effort had he wished, but who moderated his speed to conform with that of his less favored friend.

The shouts have continued all this while, proving that the citizens of Valetta have steadfastly pursued them with some dark purpose in view.

Just as soon as Philander Sharpe makes this discovery, his action is one that proves him a hero.

He stops in his tracks, and no longer keeps up his flight.

"Turn the other way, boys! At 'em like thunder! As Sheridan said at Cedar Creek: 'We'll lick 'em out of their boots,'" is the astonishing cry he sends forth, as he begins to travel over the back trail.

This speedily brings him upon the scene of action. Several dark figures have come to a halt around a prostrate object. They are the men of Valetta, who have organized this secret vendetta against all foreigners.

It is easy to understand why they thus halt. John Craig is the recumbent, struggling figure on the roadway; John Craig, who has possibly been lassoed by some expert among the pursuers, and who kicks with the vim and energy of a free American citizen.

St. George Rathborne

This Philander understands instantly, and also comprehending that he must do something very speedily, throws himself into the midst of the dusky Maltese thugs.

The advent of a wild-cat could not produce more astonishment and consternation than this sudden coming of the energetic little man.

He accompanies his assault with the most energetic movements of both arms and legs, and his shrill voice keeps time to the music.

As he holds the cimeter-knife in one hand, his movements are not without certain painful accompaniments. The men fall back in dismay. A momentary panic is upon them. Philander is shrewd enough to know this will not last, and he does not attempt to pursue them.

Upon finding that for the time being the scene is left to him, and that he is the master of the situation, the professor bends down to free his companion from the noose that binds his arms.

Already has John managed to gain a sitting posture, as the fellow at the other end of the rope forgets to pull steadily upon it in his alarm at the new phase of affairs.

Before he can collect his wits, and once more stretch the line, Philander's keen blade of Damascus steel is pressed against the rope, and as it comes taut it instantly separates.

This is enough for John, who has now gained his feet, and throws aside the entangling loop.

His tumble has had a queer effect on the young doctor; usually cool and cautious, he has been transformed into a

Hotspur; there is a sudden desire for revenge.

In his hand he holds a cudgel, which he snatched from the street as he arose. It is the spoke of a wheel belonging to some light vehicle, and which no doubt one of the assailants carried.

With this flourishing about his head, Doctor Chicago leaps in among the Maltese and belabors them right and left.

As Philander, seeing what is going on, and knowing his assistance would be appreciated, springs to his side, the dusky sons of Malta break and run.

They realize, perhaps, that they have waked up the wrong customers, and immediate flight is the only thing that will save them from the result of their impetuosity.

The two Americans make a pretense of pursuing them, but truth to tell their course really lies in an altogether different direction, and, as if by mutual consent, they suddenly turn right about face.

Taking advantage of the enemy's discomfiture, they are enabled to make good their escape, and presently reach the vicinity of the hotel, rather out of breath, and looking somewhat the worse for their strange adventures.

Professor Sharpe has been glowing with pride and satisfaction up to the moment they reach the caravansary, then all of a sudden he seems to collapse.

A sound comes from a window above; a clear, sibilant sound; a human voice uttering one word, but investing it with a volume of reproach beyond description.

That word:

"Philander!"

The doughty little professor, who has proved himself as brave as a lion in the face of actual and overwhelming danger, now shows positive signs of flunking. He clutches the arm of his fellow-adventurer, and whispers:

"John Craig, remember your solemn promise."

"Never fear; I'll stand by you, professor."

"Philander Sharpe!"

This time the inflection is more positive and acrid. It is no longer a tone of plaint and entreaty, but touches the Caudle lecture style. Of course, he can no longer ignore the presence of his better half.

"It's I, Gwendolin," he says, meekly.

"Oh, it is! You've condescended to take some notice of me at last. Well, I'm glad to see you. Come up stairs at once, and confess that you've treated me abominably, you bad man."

"For Heaven's sake let's get in before a crowd gathers," groans the professor, with a glance of horror up in the direction of the white-capped head protruding from, the second-story window.

Craig is amused, but takes pity on his companion, so they enter the hotel together.

"Will you tell her all?" he asks.

"She'll never rest content now until she discovers it," says Philander, sadly.

"Then make a clean breast. I give you permission to speak of my affairs, only—"

"What?"

"Somehow I'd rather not have Lady Ruth know about Pauline Potter, and the foolish whim that causes her to pursue me."

At this Philander chuckles, being able to see through a millstone with a hole in it.

"I'll warn Gwendolin, then. She entertains a warm feeling for you, John—always has since making your acquaintance; and after the event of to-day, or rather yesterday, since it is past the witching hour of midnight, she is ready to do anything for you."

"Well, good-night, professor," with a warm shake of the hand, for what they have passed through in common to-night will make these two the best of friends.

When John Craig finds himself alone, he does not at once retire to his small room. Sleep is one of the last things he thinks of just at present, his mind has been so wrought up by the events of the night.

The hotel remains open. It is not customary, for there are no late trains to come in at Valetta, and the people keep early hours, as a usual thing, but this is an exceptional time of the year, preceding Lent, and there may be some other reason besides that causes an all-night open house.

St. George Rathborne

Doctor Chicago finds a chair, and seats himself, first of all to reflect upon the singular train of events that has marked a red cross in his career since the last sunrise.

His stricken arm pains him, but he has not the slightest fear as to the ultimate outcome of that episode; the self-inflicted scorching with the hot iron effectually ended that.

At last he draws out the piece of paper which Philander secured in the room that marked their downfall, the paper that bears the signature of Sister Magdalen.

Lady Ruth's reminiscence has thus proved of great value to him.

He takes out one of the notes which came periodically to him—it is the one that bore the postmark of Valetta, Malta. Holding the two side by side, he eagerly compares them.

"Yes, the same hand penned both—I would swear to that."

Long he muses, sitting there. The papers have been put away, his cigar falls unheeded to the floor, and his thoughts fly far away.

Finally he arises, with a sigh, and seeks his room, to rest very poorly, between the pain of his arm and the worry of his mind.

Another day dawns upon Valetta.

As yet the tourists, who sojourn at the city of Malta by the sea, have received no intimation that the disabled steamer is in a condition to proceed.

This means another day on the island, for which few are

really sorry, as Valetta is not an unpleasant place in winter.

Our friends gather around the breakfast-table, and conversation is brisk. More than once Lady Ruth watches the face
of John Craig. She is anxious to hear what success he met
with on the preceding night, and will doubtless find an
opportunity for a quiet little chat after the meal.

On his part, Craig is uneasy, feeling that he owes her a
recital of facts, and yet loth to tell her anything about Pauline
Potter, for he is ashamed of his boyish infatuation with
regard to the Chicago actress.

So he dallies over his breakfast, hoping that something will
turn up to lead their thoughts in another channel, and at least
give them a longer respite. Perhaps a message will come
from the steamer announcing an immediate sailing.

He is eager to be off. Whatever was in the note Philander
picked up in the house of the Strada Mezzodi, it has given
John a feverish anxiety to reach some other port.

Ah! here is the good captain of the Hyperion himself, a jolly
sea-dog whom every passenger clings to in time of storm and
trouble, and who buoys up trembling souls, fearful of the
worst, with his hearty, good-natured manner.

He announces aloud for the benefit of his passengers that a
notice just posted in the office of the hotel gives the time of
the vessel's sailing at seven in the evening, and all passengers
are requested to be on board before that hour, if possible.

This means another day on shore. It means that John Craig
cannot longer elude the recital of his night's adventures to
Lady Ruth.

CHAPTER X

SPRUNG ALEAK!

Lady Ruth captures him very soon after breakfast by means of a clever little piece of diplomacy. John is really amused at the manner in which she manages this affair, and allows himself to be carried off to enjoy a bird's-eye view of the harbor which she has discovered at the end of the piazza, and which he must pass an opinion upon.

The others do not follow, Philander and Aunt Gwen, because they know what is going on, and Sir Lionel, on account of a bore of a British nobleman who has fastened upon him, and talks an incessant streak.

Miss Caprice, as Aunt Gwen has christened Lady Ruth, suddenly develops a new phase in the conversation.

"Do you know what time it was when you came in last night?" she says, shaking a finger at him, whereat John laughingly declares his ignorance, having failed to take note of it.

"Just a quarter of two."

"Is it possible? Really, I—"

"Now, it would be only justice to myself to tell how I happened to know. Awaking from sleep with a slight head-ache, I arose to get my smelling-salts, and noted the time.

"Just then I heard Aunt Gwen's angelic voice calling down. My first fear was that Uncle Philander had gone off on some sort of racket, and was returning in no condition for a gentleman, for which suspicion I humbly beg his pardon, for he's just as lovely as a man ever could be."

"A fine little fellow, I'll declare, and he stood by me like a hero," declares John, with great earnestness.

"Well, I'm a woman, you know, and curious. I poked my head out of the window, and saw that you were with the professor. Of course, I knew he was all right, then."

The charming *naivette* with which she makes this engaging remark almost takes John's breath away. He feels a mad desire to take her in his arms, and to call her "you blessed darling," or some other similarly foolish pet name.

Fortunately he contents himself with putting his feelings into a burning look, the ardor of which causes the cheeks of the young ma'mselle to grow as red as fire, and she looking the other way at the time.

"I promised to tell you what success I had in my search," he begins, knowing the confession to be inevitable.

Now she looks at him eagerly, expectantly.

"Yes, and I have tried to read the result in your face, but fear that it has not been flattering."

So he tells her all, dealing lightly with the matter of Miss

Pauline, though she is such an important factor in the game that she cannot be ignored.

Lady Ruth looks him directly in the eyes with her own steel blue orbs, so honest, so strong, that John has always delighted to meet their gaze, nor does he avoid it now.

"Perhaps I have no business to ask, Doctor Craig, but this Pauline Potter—what is she to you, what was she to you that she goes to all this trouble? Have you a secret of hers which she desires to gain?"

"I desire to retain your good opinion, Lady Ruth, and conesquently am anxious that you should know all. I shall not spare myself one iota."

So he explains how the fascinating actress caught his boyish fancy some two years previous, and how devoted he had been to her until he learned of her duplicity.

Then followed his denunciation in the presence of several admirers, after which he had not seen her again until the night before.

All of which is told in a frank way, and listened to with earnestness.

At the conclusion of his narrative, John looks again into Lady Ruth's face to see whether she condemns him or not, and is gratified to discover a smile there.

"I think you are little to blame, Doctor Chicago. Like all young men, you were dazzled by the bright star that flashed before your eyes; but your illusion lasted only a brief time, for which you may be thankful. As to this woman's endeavor to regain your regard, it shows what a brazen creature she is."

The fine contempt she feels is written on her face, and John is glad he made a full confession of the whole matter.

"I hope I will never see her again," he says, in a penitent way.

"So do I," she echoes, and then turns a trifle red, hastily adding: "for your sake, doctor. Now, tell me what you hope to do about finding your mother."

Thus, with the diplomacy of a general, upon finding herself growing uncomfortable she instantly changes the situation, and brings a new question to the fore.

John does not notice this. He is too well pleased with the fact that she overlooks his indiscretion, and still grants him her valued friendship.

He goes on to explain his plans.

They are not elaborate. The paper which Philander Sharpe discovered gives him a new clew, and this he means to push to the utmost.

He anticipates success, but is gradually learning to tone down his enthusiasm, realizing that difficulties beset his way.

Thus all has been told, and he has not lost rating with the proud English girl, for whose good opinion he is coming to be solicitous.

Presently Aunt Gwen is heard calling her niece, and they think it time to join the rest, as the plans of the day are being discussed.

St. George Rathborne

There are still many things to be seen on the Island of Malta by the curious. A few even start for the city of Civita Vecchia in the center of the island, but our friends decide against such an expedition, as there is a chance of delay, and the captain may refuse to hold his vessel an hour longer than is absolutely necessary.

Again they start out, and in seeing various curious things the day is gradually passed.

John is glad that no sign is discovered that would indicate the presence of Pauline Potter near them.

He has feared lest the vindictive actress might take it into her head to suddenly appear, and publicly denounce him as her recreant lover, and thinking thus, is especially glad that he told Lady Ruth the whole story.

So the day ends.

It has been a remarkably pleasant one to all of them, and John has certainly enjoyed it to the utmost. When I say all, there should be an exception, for Sir Lionel is in anything but an angelic frame of mind.

He has been wont to look upon the young American's chances with regard to winning Lady Ruth as exceedingly slim, when such a hero as himself enters the field.

That is an Englishman's egotism sure enough. To him Doctor Chicago seems only a boy, and he looks upon John's daring to enter the lists against him as a specimen of Yankee assurance.

This day teaches Sir Lionel that nothing can account for the vagaries of a girl's mind. She even shows a decided preference for the society of the American, allows him to carry her parasol, to assist her up the steps when they visit the signal tower, and on several occasions they manage to slip off by themselves, and can be seen eagerly comparing notes and exchanging opinions respecting the magnificent views that are to be suddenly discovered at various points.

The British soldier is too old a campaigner not to know what all this signifies, though the bull-dog elements in his composition will not let him dream of giving up as yet.

"It's all owing to that beastly little affair of yesterday. The boy made a big jump in her estimation, when he saved that child. It was a brave act. I don't want to say a word to the contrary, and the lad has grit, more than I ever dreamed of; but I want Lady Ruth, by Jove, more than I ever wanted anything in all my life, and as I've said before, when a British soldier fails to succeed one way, he will another."

Thinking thus, Sir Lionel cudgels his brains during the day, in order to invent some *coup de grace* by means of which he may cleverly regain his lost prestige.

When a man allows his passions to get the better of his judgment and sense of fair play, he is really but a single step from being a scoundrel, and although Sir Lionel would have vehemently scouted the suspicion of his doing anything to sully his fair name, he nevertheless, in his desperation at being worsted in a love affair by a mere boy, goes about some things that are hardly fair.

It has been decided that the little party shall go aboard after supper, by the light of the young moon, which will be nearly overhead.

Two boats have been engaged to wait for them at the quay.

It is at this time Sir Lionel hopes to make his point, and to accomplish it he does not hesitate to descend to a low plane, and even imperil human life.

When they reach the quay a breeze is blowing, but not strong enough to cause any uneasiness.

The party place their luggage in one boat.

Then comes a pretty piece of by-play that really reflects credit upon the engineering skill of the soldier, for it is his hand that pulls the strings.

Lady Ruth steps into one boat. One of the men having stopped John to ask him something, the colonel is given a chance to occupy the same boat, and, when Doctor Chicago arrives, he is told by the boatman that this craft having two passengers, and being smaller than the other, can carry no more.

Sir Lionel as they push off sings out to him, pleasantly:

"A Roland for an Oliver, Chicago."

John smothers his chagrin and enters the other, boat with Aunt Gwen and the professor. After all, it is only for a brief time, and surely he can afford to give Sir Lionel that pleasure.

Thus they set out.

Lady Ruth appears to be in good spirits, for they can hear her voice in song, blending with the bass of the baronet, floating over the waves, which are really rougher than any of them had anticipated.

The lights of the steamer can be seen, and they head for her.

Suddenly the song ceases to float across the water. It comes so suddenly to a stop that John Craig sits up in the other boat and clutches the arm of the professor.

"Listen! I thought I heard a slight scream."

"Nonsense!" exclaims Aunt Gwen.

"That British prig—"

"Sir Lionel is a gentleman. He would not sully his reputation by a word or deed."

"There—again."

"That time I heard it, too. Boatman, bend to your oars, and pull. There is something wrong with the other boat," cries the professor.

Then across the bounding waters comes a hail, in the lion-like voice of the Briton. A hail that stirs the blood in their veins until it runs like molten lava—a hail that tells of danger.

"Ho! there, this way, quick! We're sinking! sprung aleak!"

Such is the cry that comes to them.

All are at once alarmed. The boatman is pulling well, but, to John's excited fancy, it seems as though they hardly move.

He springs up, and takes one of the oars.

"Professor, mind the helm!" he cries.

St. George Rathborne

"Ay, ay!" sings out that worthy, adapting himself immediately to the situation.

The young American is hardly an athlete, although he belongs to one of Chicago's best boat clubs.

He has an incentive now which causes him to strain every muscle, and under the united strength of two men the boat dances over the billows in the quarter whence the cry of help was heard.

It nevertheless takes them nearly five minutes to reach the scene, and this is the longest five minutes John ever knew.

Only the voice of the boatman is heard, still calling, and by this they know that the climax has already come.

A dreadful fear almost palsies John's heart as they reach the scene.

The boatman is discovered, clinging to the oars, and showing some evidence of alarm. Perhaps he has had more than he bargained for.

John helps him in.

"Where are the others?" he cries, hoarsely.

"I am afraid, lost."

"Just Heaven! What has happened?"

"Boat sprung leak—go down fast. Soldier say he save lady, but struck his head on boat and lose senses. I saw them no more."

It is horrible!

"Did the boat sink?" asks John, huskily.

"I do not know."

"Would it sink under such circumstances?" he asks their own boatman, who also has the appearance of being rattled. When they entered into a little trickery with Sir Lionel, they had no idea it would turn out so tragically, and the possible serious consequences now staring them in the face make them uneasy.

"No; it could not," returns that worthy.

"Then, if floating still, we must find it. Our only chance lies there."

Fortunately John is, in a measure, self-possessed. He at least shows himself equal to the emergency.

They pull in the direction where it is most likely they will find what they seek.

John twists his neck as he rows, and endeavors to scan the sea around them. Again and again he calls out, hoping in the fullness of his heart that some answering cry may come back.

What leaden seconds those are—never can they forget them.

"I see something!" says Aunt Gwen, who is crouching in the bow, regardless of the spray that now and then spatters her.

"Where away?" demands John, eagerly.

"Straight ahead."

They pull with fierce energy.

"Can you make it out?"

"It's the swamped boat," replies Aunt Gwen, who has remarkable eyes for one of her age.

John shouts again.

"Boat ahoy!"

This time an answer comes back, but not in the roar of the British lion.

"Here—come quickly—I am nearly worn-out!"

John's heart gives a great bound.

"Thank Heaven! It is Lady Ruth!" he says.

CHAPTER XI

AN UNWELCOME PASSENGER

John can hold back no longer, but gives his oar to the boatman, and seeks the bow in place of Aunt Gwen, who allows him the privilege.

They are now almost upon the floating swamped boat.

"Careful now. Don't run into the wreck. I see her," and with the last words, John, who has kicked off his shoes in almost a second of time, throws coat and vest down in the boat and leaps overboard.

His hands seize upon the gunwale of the nearly submerged boat, over which each wave breaks. He pulls himself along, and thus reaches Lady Ruth whom he finds holding on to one of the tiller ropes which has formed a loop, through which her arm is passed.

"Thank Heaven! You are safe! Here comes the boat! You must let me help you in, Lady Ruth!" he says, dodging a wave and ready to clutch her if she lets go.

"I am not alone. You must take him in first," she gasps.

Then John for the first time becomes aware that she is supporting Sir Lionel, whose arm has also been passed through the rounded tiller rope.

He seems to hang a dead weight.

Amazed at the action of the brave English girl, John at once takes hold of the soldier. The boat by this time comes up.

In getting him aboard a spill is narrowly averted, and now a new trouble arises. The boat will hold no more, and is dangerously loaded even now.

What can be done? Lady Ruth must be taken aboard. Her strength is almost gone, and John, in deadly fear lest one of the hungry waves should tear her away before their very eyes, passes an arm around her waist.

He takes in the situation.

"Here, you!" to the already wet boatman, "tumble overboard, quick now. We can hold on behind, I reckon."

The man hesitates, and this is a bad time for deliberation.

Professor Sharpe suddenly seizes upon him, and in almost the twinkling of an eye has the fellow overboard, more through a quick movement than any show of strength.

"There's a boat from the steamer coming this way. Hail it, Philander!" exclaims Aunt Gwen, and this gives them new life.

Lady Ruth is now taken into the boat with some degree of caution.

Sir Lionel shows no sign of life, and both ladies are extremely solicitous about him, so the professor bends down to make a cursory examination.

"He'll be all right when the water is pumped out of him," he announces.

The boat from the steamer comes up, led to the spot by Philander's shrill whoops, and the men in the water are rescued.

In ten minutes they reach the side of the steamer and go aboard. A terrible disaster has been narrowly averted, and John cannot but feel amazed at the wonderful grit shown by this girl, who saved the baronet from a watery grave.

It proves his estimation of her qualities at the time she assisted to bind up his arm was not out of the way.

As the two boatmen are about to go down into their craft again, the one who has not been in the water beckons John, who has not yet sought his cabin-room to change his soaked clothes.

"Will the gentleman recover?" he asks.

"You mean Sir Lionel? Oh, yes! He is already back in his senses. Strangely enough the first question he asked upon learning that Lady Ruth was saved, concerned your companion, and when he learned that the boatman had also survived, he said: 'The devil!'"

At this the man chuckles.

"I understand—perhaps you can. I like you, sir, while his ways make me mad. He thinks we Maltese dogs. I say no more—only look out for him. It easy to sink when plank in boat loosened."

Without another word the fellow slides down the rope to his boat, and pushes off with his soaked companion.

When John turns and heads for his state-room, he has something to think about, and the consciousness that there has been some foul play about this accident makes him decidedly uneasy.

Now they are off, the passengers who in the morning started on a pilgrimage to Civita Vecchia having returned in good time.

When Doctor Chicago once more comes on deck, clad in warm, dry clothes, the lights of Valetta are astern, and the steamer is putting miles between them.

He paces up and down, reflecting upon the startling event of the evening.

What can the significant words of the boatman mean, if not what he suspects.

John would not wrong any one, and he believes it policy to keep this to himself. At the same time he realizes that the game is taking on a desperate phase, when a gentleman of Sir Lionel's caliber descends to such treachery, in order to make himself a favorite with the fair English maid.

Of course, it was his intention to save Lady Ruth and appear the hero. He trusted in his well-known ability as an expert swimmer to accomplish this, and never once thought fate would step in and deal him such a blow.

As near as can be learned from what the wet boatman said when picked up, just when the craft was sinking Sir Lionel must have stumbled and fallen, striking his head upon the gunwale, which rendered him unconscious.

John walks up and down, smoking and pondering, and, when his thoughts go toward Lady Ruth, he smiles as if they are pleasant.

Twice he goes to seek the stewardess to make inquiries concerning the young woman, and is gratified to hear that the ship's Scotch surgeon has given her a glass of warm toddy to keep her from taking cold as a result of her exposure, and that having retired she is now in a perfectly natural sleep.

Pleased with this, he lights another cigar and resumes his walk, to meet Sir Lionel, who has quite recovered from his ducking, and is disposed to treat the whole matter something like a joke.

John engages him in conversation for a purpose, and learns what he can about the peculiar affair; but the soldier professes to know nothing beyond the fact that the boatman suddenly cried that the craft was sinking, whereupon he called out for assistance from the other boat, and then, as the emergency seemed very close, he sprang up to save Lady Ruth, when his foot caught in the thwart and he pitched heavily forward.

He was not wholly unconscious, and with some one's help, he knew not whom at the time, he managed to crook his arm through the rope belonging to the tiller. After which he knew no more until he came to on board the steamer and found the surgeon pouring whisky down his throat.

"Perhaps your boatman was crazy. I'm sure our fellow must

have been out of his mind, judging from his actions when leaving the steamer. Why, he even warned me to keep an eye on you, sir."

At this the Englishman removes his cigar from between his teeth, looks hard at the doctor, says "by Jove!" several times, and then laughs heartily.

"That is very funny. Indeed, I can't remember anything that strikes me as more peculiar. Any one can watch me—my actions are, I hope, above-board. It is true I am disappointed in not having been able to have saved Lady Ruth, but so long as some one took her from the water, what does it matter? The boatmen are mad, because they lost a craft. Jove! I'd like to teach them a lesson for taking out passengers in a cranky, rotten boat. Do you know, I believe my foot went clean through the bottom when I jumped up."

This, spoken in a frank, ingenuous way, quite disarms John.

He does not like to think evil of his fellow human beings, at any rate.

The wind is increasing meanwhile, and clouds hide the young moon.

"I believe we will have a storm," is the last remark Sir Lionel makes, as he staggers across the rising deck and makes a plunge down into the cabin, for although a duck in the water, the Briton is no yachtsman, and possibly already feels the terrible grip of the coming *mal de mer*.

His words are soon verified, however, for the waves and wind continue to rise until the steamer is mightily buffeted. Still John remains on deck. There is a fascination for him in the scene that words cannot express. When he has had enough he will find his state-room and sleep, for surely he needs it after being awake a good deal of the preceding night at Valetta.

Darker grow the heavens. Thunder rolls, and the electric current cuts the air, illuminating the wild scene with a picturesque touch that is almost ghastly in its yellow white.

The steamer is well built, and in good condition to withstand the tempest, roar as it may. John tires of the weird spectacle at last, and he, too, makes a plunge for the cabin, reaching it just in time to escape a monster wave that makes the vessel stagger, and sweeps along the deck from stem to stern.

Below he finds considerable confusion, such as is always seen on board a steamer during a storm. Timid men looking as white as ghosts, frightened women wringing their hands and screaming with each plunge of the ship, as if they expect it to be the last.

A few foreign passengers are aboard, and they do not seem free from the contagion, though inclined to be more stoical than the Europeans.

As the steamer plunges, some of the passengers are huddled in a corner. Loud praying can be heard, and those who are least accustomed to such things on ordinary occasions are most vehement now.

A Mohammedan is kneeling on his rug, with his face turned in the direction of Mecca, as near as he can judge, and going through with the strange rigmarole of bows and muttered phrases that constitute his religion.

This scene is not a very pleasant one, but there are features about it which are worth being noticed, and John stands to

St. George Rathborne

gaze before seeking his room.

He has heard from the captain that the boat is perfectly safe, unless the storm should grow much heavier, and with this assurance intends to seek his berth and sleep, if such a thing be possible.

He moves toward his state-room. Just then a billow strikes the steamer almost amidships, and she rolls. This, not being expected, causes John to slide across the cabin floor, to the accompaniment of a chorus of cries from the frightened people, who are huddled in a corner by this new move on the part of the vessel.

He brings up alongside a state-room door, which is in the act of being opened, even as he bangs up against it.

Consequently John has the greatest difficulty in maintaining his balance, and in order to keep from sliding through the door grasps the sides.

Some one has opened it. A face is exposed close to his own, a face that, although not terror-stricken, bears the evidence of sudden alarm, as though the new pitch of the vessel and renewed shrieks from within have aroused fear—a face that John Craig recognizes with amazement.

"Tell me, are we sinking?" she exclaims.

Then she looks again.

"Ah! Doctor Chicago!"

"You here, Pauline Potter?"

The presence of the actress on board the steamer gives him a sudden thrill.

It is no mere accident that brings her, but a part of a deep-laid plan, which perhaps not only concerns him, but one in whom he has taken the deepest interest—Lady Ruth.

That is why he cries out, and his words have more than an ordinary amount of astonishment in them.

"Yes, I am leaving Malta. I have no reason to remain there longer. But tell me the worst, John Craig; are we doomed to go down?"

The vessel does not toss so wildly now, and the wails of the alarmed passengers grow less in volume.

"I hope not. The captain assured me there was no danger whatever, and told me to get some sleep, if I could. I am on my way to my berth now. Be of good cheer, the morning will see us safe enough, I believe."

Then he leaves her, and the state-room door closes.

This encounter makes John think of the other ladies. Are Aunt Gwen and Lady Ruth among those whose clamor arises from the cabin with each lurch of the ship?

As the thought flashes upon his mind, some one clutches his arm, and, turning, he beholds the little professor. There is a wild look in Philander's eyes, and his teeth rattle like castanets. Really the situation is terrible enough to appall any one.

"When do we go down, John?" he asks.

"Good Heaven! I trust not at all," and he cheers the other

with what the captain has told him.

"I wish you could tell the ladies that."

"Where are they?" asks John.

"Come with me!"

In a few seconds the doctor sees the ladies, who have a state-room together. They are fully dressed, and look woe-begone. At each lunge of the vessel they gasp, and, when a particularly big one occurs, fall into each other's arms.

Both are brave enough, and yet the situation is such that a strange feeling creeps over the stoutest heart.

When John appears, and tells them what the captain has said, it reassures them considerably, and they feel better.

Presently he leaves them, and seeks his berth, where he actually goes to sleep. Tired nature will assert her power, even under the most discouraging conditions.

During the night the storm abates.

John Craig is awake early, and can tell that all is well from the easy motion of the steamer, for her plunges are few and of small moment. A silence broods over the scene; the tired passengers have gone to sleep; all John can hear as he lies there is the dull throb of the engines and the swish of water against the side of the vessel.

CHAPTER XII

TO THE HOUSE OF BEN TALEB

Algiers!

The sunset gun is just booming over the African hills as the steamer drops anchor off the wonderful city where the French have gained a foothold and seem determined to stay.

John Craig is in a fever to go ashore. He has had news that from Malta his mother went to Algiers on a mission, and his one object in life is to follow her until the time comes when he can see face to face the woman to whom he owes his being, toward whom his heart goes out, and whom he believes to have been dreadfully wronged.

Most of the passengers are going farther, but as the steamer will remain in the harbor until morning, there is no need of any going ashore.

John, however, cannot wait.

He engages a boatman—there are many who at once come out to the steamer for various purposes—tells his friends where they may find him, and with his luggage is away, just before darkness sets in, for it comes very soon after sunset in

St. George Rathborne

this country.

Upon landing, John secures a guide, and makes for the central square known as the *Place du Gouvernement*, where he knows of a good hotel, recommended by the captain.

The air is fragrant with the odor of flowers.

In his walk he meets strange people, Arabs, Moors, Kabyles from the desert, long-bearded Jews, Greeks, negroes, Italians, and, of course, French soldiers.

Al Jezira, as the natives call their capital, is undoubtedly the most interesting city for a traveler's eyes, exceeding even Constantinople and Cairo.

Part of the city is modern, the rest just as it might have been a century ago, when the Algerian pirates made a reign of terror sweep over the Mediterranean.

Omnibuses are seen, and even street-cars run to Birkadeen, a suburb. The houses on the terraces of Mustapha Superieur are peopled with the nicest of French and English families, who spend the winter in this charming place.

Still, if one enters the native quarter, ascending the narrow streets where no vehicle can ever come, where the tall, white houses, with their slits for windows, almost meet above, shutting out the cheery sunlight, where one meets the Moor, the Arab, the gipsy, the negro porter, the native woman with her face concealed almost wholly from view, it would be easy to believe the city to be entirely foreign and shut off from European intercourse.

Within a stone's throw how different the scene—the wide streets, the fine houses, the people of Paris and London mixing with the picturesque costumes of the natives, the bazaars, music in the air coming from the Kasbah, once the stronghold of the merciless Janizaries, now the barracks for French zouaves, the bric-a-brac merchant with his extraordinary wares spread out, while he calmly smokes a cigarette and plays upon the mandolin.

No wonder the pilgrim in Algiers is charmed, and lingers long beyond his time.

John has glimpses of these things on his way to the hotel, and although his mind is hardly in a condition to take much notice of such matters, they nevertheless impress him to a certain degree.

Dull, indeed, must be the man who cannot grasp the wonderful beauty of such a scene. At another time John would have been charmed.

He reaches the hotel, and at once engages a room. Supper is ready, and he sits down to a meal one can hardly procure outside of Paris itself, and served in French style.

If any one were watching John, his nervousness would be perceptible.

From the table he seeks the office of the hotel.

"What can I do for monsieur?" asks the polite attendant, seeing him standing there expectantly.

"I desire to procure a guide."

"To-morrow?"

"Now—at once."

The clerk looks at him curiously. He cannot understand what such impetuosity means.

He realizes that he is dealing with one who is different from the usual run of travelers.

"Monsieur does not, perhaps, know the danger involved in the night; foreigners do not often invade the old town after dark."

"Pardon me, my business is very important. Can you procure me a reliable guide, one who speaks English?"

"It can be done. First, I would recommend that you seal up your watch and valuables in this envelope."

"A good idea. You will keep them in your safe," suiting the action to the word.

"Now; monsieur will write his name."

"Done."

"Also the address."

"Eh? I don't quite understand."

"To which he would have them sent."

"Sent?"

"In case we see monsieur no more."

"Ah! Now I catch on," with a smile, as he adds the words: "Chicago, Ill., U.S.A."

"Chicago, I have heard of it; quite a place," remarks the clerk.

"Rather," dryly. "The cicerone, please."

Then the clerk beckons to a man who has been lounging not far away.

John sweeps his eyes over him.

He sees an Arab gipsy, a swarthy fellow of stalwart build, dressed in the attractive costume of his race. John reads human nature fairly well, and he believes he sees a man who can be depended on.

"This, monsieur, is Mustapha Cadi. You can depend upon him always," and the clerk goes to his regular work.

The Arab makes the ordinary salutation, crossing his hands over his breast, and bowing.

These people are very ceremonious, never entering a room or being seated before a guest.

"You speak English?" asks John.

"Oh, yes!" smiling.

"I want to engage you in my service for some days, Mustapha Cadi."

"I have just come with a party from the wine caves of Chateau Hydra and the cemetery on Bouzareah. I am now free, and in monsieur's service."

"Good! Your terms?"

"Two duros a day."

"I will make it four."

"Great is Allah, and Mohammed is his prophet. I shall not complain."

"There is a condition."

"Name it."

"I am very anxious to see some one whom I have reason to believe is in this city."

"Of course."

"You must take me to him to-night."

Mustapha Cadi looks a little anxious.

"Does this illustrious person live in new or old Al Jezira?"

"I cannot say, it is for you to tell."

"His name?"

"Ben Taleb."

The Arab shrugs his shoulders, a French trick that follows their conquests, and is so very suggestive.

"The Moorish doctor; he lives in the heart of the old town."

"But many Europeans visit him, he has a reputation abroad."

"They never dare go at night."

"I am willing to take the risk."

Mustapha Cadi looks at the young man admiringly—curiously, for he cannot imagine what would cause such haste. He sees a specimen of healthy manhood, so that it can hardly be for medical advice he takes such chances to see the old Moor.

"Monsieur, I consent."

"It is well."

"I, too, have conditions."

"Ah! that may alter the case," suspiciously.

"My reputation is dear to me."

"Naturally."

"It is my means of earning much money. Listen to me. I have taken Franks everywhere through this country, to Oran and even the far-away lead mines of Jebel Wanashrees; yes, once even to the city of Fez, in Morocco; yet never has anything serious happened to those in my charge. We have been attacked by robbers in the desert, but we dispersed them with gun and yataghan. Here in Al Jezira, many times, beggars for backsheesh have become impudent, and tried to enforce their demands, but I have taken them before the cadi, and had them punished with the bastinado. Ah! they know Mustapha Cadi, the guide, and give him a wide berth *by daylight*. But, monsieur, what might happen in the streets of the old town should a Frank go there at night, I am afraid to say."

"Still, you promised."

"Ay, and will keep my word, if the monsieur agrees to the condition."

"Let me hear it!"

"I will procure a burnoose, you shall put the robe on, and be an Arab for to-night."

John draws a breath of relief, he smiles.

"Willingly, Mustapha. Let us lose no time, I beg of you!"

"Then, monsieur, come!"

As he passes the clerk that worthy bends forward to say:

"Does monsieur know these people who have come from the steamer?"

John sees a list of names under his own.

Professor Sharpe and wife. Lady Ruth Stanhope. Colonel Lionel Blunt. Miss Pauline Potter.

There they are, all present, and he hears the voice of Aunt Gwen in the dining-room, even at the moment of his reading her name, gently chiding a waiter for not serving the professor more promptly, always in a hurry, but generally good-natured withal.

"They are friends of mine," he says, and then follows his Arab guide.

Once on the street John observes what is passing around him, and the scene on the grand square is certainly lively enough, with the garrison band discoursing sweet music, the numerous lights from *cafe* and *magasius de nouveautes*, and crowds moving about.

Presently they come to a bazaar, where every article known to oriental ingenuity, from Zanzibar carpets, embroideries of Tunis, Damascus cutlery, and odd jewelry to modern novelties can be found.

Here they enter.

The guide selects what he needs, and John pays for it, wondering what sort of clumsiness he will display in the wearing of an Arab costume.

Until they reach the border of the old town upon the hillside, there is little need of his donning the ridiculous affair.

He casts many inquisitive glances upon his guide and other Arabs whom they meet to see how they wear the burnoose.

"I reckon John Craig won't disgrace Chicago, if he isn't to the manner born," he concludes.

"Now, monsieur will allow me," says his tall guide, leading him into a dark corner.

There is some little difficulty experienced, but in the end John turns Arab.

"Say not one word—if saluted, I will reply," is the last caution he receives.

Then they move on.

Now their road ascends.

They are in Al Jezira, the old Arab town.

The passage is so narrow that at times John could easily touch the walls of the spectral houses on either side by extending his arms.

Every little while there is a short step. Now and then an arch from which hangs a queer lantern, burning dimly. Over a door, here and there, a light marks the residence of some Moor or Arab of note. But for these the passage-way would be totally dark, even on the brightest moonlight night.

They meet bearded and turbaned Arabs, who stalk majestically along, proud as Lucifer, even without a piastre in their purses—even women vailed as usual, wearing anklets, and with their nails stained with henna.

The men salute, and Mustapha replies, while the disguised young American merely bows his head, which he has hidden after the manner of one who mourns.

Thus they advance.

Presently they turn sharply to the left, and enter a dark passage.

"We will wait here a few minutes."

"But why?" asks the impatient doctor.

"You saw the group above descending, monsieur?"

"Yes."

"I recognized them as rival couriers. If they saw me they would glance sharply at my companion. Perhaps for much duros they have some time taken a Frank through Al Jezira at night. That would not count. If they believed I did the same thing they would spread the news abroad, and I am afraid we would have trouble. Better a little delay than that," and he draws a finger across John's throat to signify the terrible stroke of a vengeful yataghan.

"I think you are right," replies John.

They hear the group go by, laughing and joking, and the passage is again clear.

"Again, forward, monsieur," whispers the faithful courier, and leaving their hiding-place they push on.

They are in the heart of the old town, and a most singular sensation comes over John as he looks all around to see the white walls, the solemn figures moving about, and hears sounds that never before greeted his ears.

It is as if he were in another world.

While he thus ponders and speculates, his companion comes to a sudden halt. They are at the door of a house a little more conspicuous than its fellows, and Mustapha hastily gives the rapper a resonant clang.

CHAPTER XIII

A NIGHT IN ALGIERS

His manner gives the man from Chicago to understand that he has cause for sudden anxiety.

"What is it, Mustapha?" he whispers.

"Monsieur did not notice. Two Arabs, one a *muezzin*, or priest, just passed us. They brushed against you. Perhaps they disturbed the burnoose; at any rate, their heads go together; they appear excited; they stop below; see, you can yourself notice; two more join them; they point this way. Ah! there is trouble, monsieur. Nay, do not draw a weapon; it comes not now, but later. I hear footsteps within, the bolt is withdrawn, the door opens."

What Mustapha says is true; the heavy door, still secured by a stout chain, opens half a foot, and by the dim light a Moorish lad is seen.

To him the guide addresses himself. Whatever he says in the Moorish tongue, it must be direct to the point, for immediately the door is opened wide enough to admit them, after which it is shut and the heavy bolt shoots into its socket.

John follows his conductor. For the time being he loses sight of Mustapha, and must depend upon his own abilities. Trust a young man from Chicago to be equal to any occasion, no matter how extraordinary.

In another minute he is ushered into a large room, which is decorated in an oriental way that John has never seen equaled.

Rich colors blend, soft light falls upon the many articles of a connoisseur's collection, and, taken in all, the scene is dazzling.

He gives it one glance.

Then his attention is riveted upon the figures before him. A couple of servants wait upon the owner of the house, Ben Taleb, the Moorish doctor. He is a venerable man, with white hair and a long snowy beard—his costume is simply black; but beside him sits his daughter, and she presents a spectacle John never saw equaled.

Silks of the loveliest hues, velvets that are beyond descryption, diamonds that flash and dazzle, strings of milky pearls that cause one's eyes to water. John sees the beautiful dreamy face, and thinks, as he compares it with the rosy-cheeked, laughing eyed English girl's, that these Moors make veritable dolls of their daughters.

Fortunately that Chicago assurance, which has carried him through many singular scenes, does not desert him now.

He has never yet beheld what beauty the miserable yashmak and foutah of the vailed Moorish lady concealed, and is naturally taken aback by the disclosure, but, recovering himself, he advances toward those who seem to await some

St. George Rathborne

action on his part.

The miserable burnoose he has discarded in the hall, so that, hat in hand, John now appears under his own colors.

Bowing low, much after the salaam of a native, in deference to beauty's presence, he addresses the Moorish doctor.

An observant traveler, Craig has a way of assimilating what he sees, and hence speaks in something of the figurative and flowery style so common among the dark-skinned people of all oriental countries, for an Arabian robber will be as polite as a French dandy, and apologize for being compelled to cut your throat.

Having, therefore, asked pardon for an intrusion at such an hour, he proceeds to business.

The old doctor has up to this time said not a word, only bowed; but now he speaks:

"Where do you come from?" he asks.

"America—Chicago," with the full belief that the *taleb* must have heard of the bustling city upon Lake Michigan.

And he is right, too, for the old Moor frowns.

"Chicago is accursed. I hate it, because it shelters an enemy to one I revere, one who saved my only child from death, when she lay with the fever at Alexandria. Your name, monsieur, and then your ailment, for I take it your case is urgent to bring you here under such risk."

"My name I have never been ashamed of. It is John Alexander Craig. My disease is one of the heart, and I believe—"

The appearance of the old Moor is such that John comes to a sudden stop—Ben Taleb's eyes are dilated—he stares at the young man in a fierce way, and his whole body appears to swell with rising emotions.

"Stop!" he thunders, and claps his hands in an excited way.

John, remembering his former experience, draws himself up in readiness for defense, nor is he surprised to see several slaves enter the room at the bidding of their master.

"This is the height of infamy, you who bear that hated name dare invade the home of Ben Taleb! I read your secret; you are not sick."

"No, no; I—"

"You come with another motive; you seek one who has long been lost, one who has suffered for years, unjustly, because of a Craig. May Allah's curses blight your footsteps."

"You mistake—"

"May Mohammed, his prophet, make your life a blank. May your days end in torment, and your nights be sleepless."

"When you are done, most illustrious *taleb*, allow me to speak. Even a dog should not be condemned unheard."

"Father, he is right; you are just, you are good; you condemn no man unheard. Let him speak; good may even come out of Chicago," says the lovely houri at the side of the Moor, and John thanks her with his eyes, mentally concluding that, after all, Moorish females, if nonentities on the street, have certain rights under their own roofs.

At this the great doctor frowns, but cannot withstand the angelic, appealing glance which his daughter bestows upon him.

"Perhaps it is so. What have you to say, you who bear that hated name? Since through the kindness of my child you are given the opportunity to speak, embrace it."

The situation is a peculiar one, and John feels that he must make the most of it.

"Illustrious Moor, listen then while I relate the reason for my presence, why for months I have searched country after country for one who ever seemed to be just beyond my reach, like a will-o'-the-wisp dancing over the swampy ground.

"The person I seek is known as Sister Magdalen. It is with no unworthy motive I would find her, Ben Taleb, for she is my mother."

At this the sheik and his daughter exchange significant glances. Perhaps something of incredulity may be discovered in their expression. Evidently they have heard but little of the story before, and only know that the troubles of the woman they revere came through a Craig.

John, having become stirred up, proceeds to tell them more of the past, and, while not caring to show emotion in the eyes of strangers, explains his feelings in the matter with a dignity that does him full justice.

While not thoroughly convinced, for he suspects there may be some artifice in this visit, the venerable Moor is inclined to look more favorably upon John.

"Perhaps you may not be so bad as I believed, but do not hope to receive news from me," is his slowly spoken remark.

John's heart sinks, he fears that after all his long search he is now to be frustrated by the stubborn will of an old man.

He even becomes eloquent in his appeal, and, while he fails to bring Ben Taleb to terms, he charms the sheik's daughter, whose lovely eyes glisten as she hears.

At last he wrings one promise from the Moor, to the effect that he will communicate with the lady in question, and stating the whole case, allow her to decide.

This is certainly fair enough, and Ben Taleb presumes to be a man who desires to do that which is right. Hence he agrees, but will not let John know whether news can be sent to him at the hotel on the morrow, or a week later. He must learn to practice the divine art of patience, and bide his time.

This, while a keen disappointment with regard to what he had expected and hoped for, is the best that can be done under the circumstances.

John is something of a philosopher.

When he has done his best, he is willing to trust the rest to fortune.

So he assumes a cheerfulness he is far from feeling, and assures Ben Taleb he will always be indebted to him for his kindness. After this he begs for a piece of paper, and the sheik sends one of his slaves for it. John writes a line upon it, a line that comes from his heart:

"MY MOTHER: I have searched half of the world over for

you. JOHN ALEXANDER CRAIG."

If she ever reads that, the meeting will not long be delayed, he believes.

A short time is spent in the company of the sheik and his daughter, and as the young American admits that he is a doctor, the Moor shows new interest, asking various questions concerning some of the great events in the world of surgery that prove him to be a man far beyond his class, and one who keeps abreast of the times.

Finally, as the hour grows apace, John thinks it time for him to be going.

Where is his courier, the faithful Mustapha Cadi, all this while?

As he mentions him, the sheik claps his hands and the guide appears. He enters into a brief conversation with Ben Taleb in the Moorish tongue.

John rightly guesses that the guide is relating the facts concerning their reaching the house, and that he fears they may be attacked, if they leave by the same way they entered.

The old Moor smiles, and after answering, turns to the young man from Chicago.

"There is another way of leaving this place, and one of my slaves will show you. They shall not harm one who comes to see Ben Taleb, if it can be prevented."

Then comes the ceremonious leave-taking, and John manages to get through this with credit. He has undoubtedly made a deep impression on the Moorish beauty, who, catching the crumbs falling from her father's table of knowledge, has aspirations above being the wife of a Moor, who may also have a harem.

At last they start off, with the slave in the lead, and after passing through several rooms, which John views with interest, arrive at a wall.

Acting under the advice of his guide, John has assumed the burnoose again, for Mustapha carried it on his arm when he appeared.

"We will pass through this door, and reach another street. Are you ready, monsieur?"

John replies in the affirmative. The light is hidden under a basket, and then a sound is heard as of a door slowly opening.

"Pass through," whispers the guide.

Thus they reach the outside, and the wall resumes its innocent appearance. If they are fortunate, they will avoid the trouble that lay in wait at the door of the old Moor.

John no longer trembles in anticipation of what is to come. He has been disappointed, and yet bears his burden well.

His guide is yet cautious, believing that one is not safe until out of the woods. It is possible word may have been sent around among the strolling Moors and Arabs of the old town, that a Frank is wandering about in a burnoose under the care of Mustapha Cadi, and hence discovery, with its attendant desperate conflict, still to come.

By degrees they approach the boundary line, and will soon

St. George Rathborne

be safe.

John is obliged to admire the diplomatic way in which the Arab conducts the retreat it would be creditable to a military strategist. They dodge and hide, now advancing, anon secreting themselves in dark corners.

At last—success!

Into the brilliant light of the new Algiers they pass; the danger is behind, safety assured.

Then Craig turns to the Arab, and tells him in plain language what he thinks of such remarkable work, and Mustapha humbly answers that he is glad the monsieur is satisfied.

Secretly, he exults in the eulogy; for even an Arab is able to appreciate praise.

Thus they bring up at the hotel.

John looks at the hour, and finds it ten. He sees the clerk nodding, and, as he repossesses himself of his valuables, accepts the other's congratulations with respect to having gone through such an experience, and lived to tell the tale.

Where are the others?

They do not seem to be about.

The music has ceased on the square, which is less crowded than before, although many people still saunter about, fakirs cry aloud their goods, and the scene is one which has certain fascinations for the traveler's eye, a warmth of color not to be found in American cities.

Here venders of fruit drinks serve their wares in an attractive way, with queer jars and fancy glasses that lend quite an inducement to purchase.

Upon making inquiries of the clerk, he finds that his four fellow-tourists have sauntered out some time since, and as yet failed to return; so John also steps outside.

In a moment Mustapha is at his side, and what he whispers is not pleasant news:

"Monsieur must be careful. The news has gone abroad that he it was who invaded Al Jezira on this night. Some one has spread the report that he is a spy, that his mission is to discover the details of the plot that is always going on among my people, for the rescue of Algiers from French hands. Hence he is watched; they may even proceed to violence. What little I have learned tells me this. Be awake; be always ready for defense, and seek not the dark corners where an assassin might lie. Bismillah!"

This is pleasant, indeed.

John has something of the feeling that comes upon the man who awaits the verdict of the jury.

At the same time he is resolved to take the advice given, and be on his guard.

As he saunters around, he fails to see those whom he seeks, though soon becoming conscious of the fact that he is watched and followed.

This does not add to his pleasure.

From the hints Mustapha has dropped, he begins to realize

that there is some sort of a league in Al Jezira, looking toward an uprising and the coming of a patriot leader, who will take charge of the rebellion.

He has gained the ill-will of these conspirators by this night visit to the old town, and how unfortunate this may be for him, the future may prove.

It is while he wanders about the square, keeping in the light, and always on his guard, that John receives something of a shock.

He sees a figure ahead, a figure garbed as a sister. She moves slowly on, her face is vailed, and a mad impulse comes upon him to toss aside that vail, to discover whether this can be Sister Magdalen, the one for whom he searches, or another.

CHAPTER XIV

THE COMING OF MISS CAPRICE

This sudden impulse on the part of the young Chicago doctor may be the means of getting him into trouble, for no people are more quick to resent an insult, either fancied or real, to females upon the street, than those of Algeria, Egypt, or Turkey.

Woman is not an equal there, but a highly prized possession, and must never appear upon the street with her face unvailed, so that any man caught tearing the foutah of a lady from her face would be severely dealt with.

John, of course, is only desirous of seeing whether this may be his mother, but the public will hardly take this fact into consideration.

Upon so suddenly conceiving this bold plan of action, John Craig hastens his footsteps, and there is need of hurry, if he hopes to overtake the figure in black before she leaves the square, for, as if conscious that she is pursued, she has also quickened her pace.

He overhauls her just on the outskirts of the Place du Gouvernement, and as he brushes past quickly raises his

St. George Rathborne

hand to snatch aside the flowing vail.

Again his heart almost stands still, and the sacred word "mother" trembles on his lips, as he bends forward to get a quick glance of the face that must be disclosed by the shifting of the vail.

His quick movement is not without its result. The vail is drawn aside, and John Craig receives a staggering blow as he gazes upon the shriveled countenance of an old woman.

It is impossible that this can be his mother—perish the thought!—and yet the garb is one seldom seen on the streets of Algiers.

His almost palsied hand drops the vail. Lucky for him will it be if no jealous Moor's eyes have seen the action.

The Sister does not cry out, and call upon those who are present to avenge the insult—even had she been a Moorish lady, the demand for punishment would not come from her, but from those of the sterner sex near-by.

Instead, she stands there as if waiting for him to speak—stands there like a statue in black.

John at once apologizes for his rudeness—he is already sorry for what he has done.

"Madame, pardon. I believed you were one very dear to me, one who wears the insignia of your order, one for whom I have searched far and near, half the world over—my mother."

"It was a bold act, young sir, but far be it from me to denounce you. Tell me, how would you know this mother?"

she asks, in a thick voice.

"She is known as Sister Magdalen—perhaps you know her—she may even be staying at the same convent as yourself," eagerly.

"I know one Sister Magdalen, a sweet, quiet woman, lately from Malta, whither she went to consult the head of our order."

Her words arouse John.

"It is she. If you would only take me to her, I would at once be rid of all these doubts and fears."

"Would you come?"

John has forgotten the warning of Mustapha, forgotten all former experiences. There is a crowd gathering around them, and this is one of the things he was to guard against, still he pays little attention to this fact, his mind is so bent upon accomplishing his object.

"Eagerly. Once this night I have risked much to find my mother, and I am ready to do more."

"Then follow me. Better still, walk at my side, for I see ugly faces around. You have made enemies, but I will stand between. My garb is sacred, and they will respect it."

"I am ready, lead on."

What is this that plucks at his sleeve? He half-turns impatiently, and looks into a face he ought to know full well, but which he now sees with something of annoyance.

"Ah! professor, is it you? Sorry—in something of a hurry—"

"Hold on; some one wants to see you."

"Have to do later."

"Don't say so, John. Important, I tell you."

"So is this. Good-by."

The professor is not so easily shaken off, but tightens his hold. John will have to dislodge him by muscular force.

"Are you coming?" asks the Sister.

"Yes, when I have broken loose from the hands of this madman."

He turns upon the professor.

"John, be careful. Cool off; you are excited."

"I'm of an age to take care of myself. When I need a guardian, I'll call on you. Once more I say, release your grasp."

He actually looks ugly for the moment, and Philander does let go, but it is only because, as an advance courier, he has accomplished his mission, and not on account of any fear.

As Doctor Chicago turns to follow the Sister, he draws in a long breath, for he finds himself face to face with Lady Ruth.

She has hurried up behind Philander, and near-by can be seen the British soldier and Aunt Gwen, also pushing forward as rapidly as the assembling crowd will allow.

"Doctor Craig."

Her presence recalls John to his senses.

"I am going to see my mother, Lady Ruth," he says, as if apologizing for his rudeness.

"With whom?"

"This Sister."

Lady Ruth surveys the other from her vail to the hem of her dress.

"I would advise you not to do so, doctor."

"Why do you say that?" he asks, astonished.

"Because you will regret it, because you are being made the victim of another plot."

"Lady Ruth, do I hear aright? Do you fully realize what it is you say?"

"I am conscious of the gravity of the charge, but that does not prevent me from asserting it. I repeat what I said before, that you are again the victim of a plot. As to this Sister here, can it be possible you do not know her?"

He shakes his head.

"Have you seen her face?"

"It is old and shriveled—that of a stranger."

At this the Sister throws back her vail, and they see the

features John describes.

"After all I am right," says John, with the air of a man who attempts to justify himself.

At that the English girl laughs scornfully.

"Really, I did not think men could be so easily deceived, and one whom I considered as shrewd as you, Doctor Chicago. See what a miserable deception, a fraud transferred from the boards of a New York theater to Algiers. Behold! the magic wand touches age with a gentle touch, and what follows?"

Lady Ruth is standing between the two, and within arm's length of either.

The Sister has not moved, but, as if confident of influencing John, holds her own. She shoots daggers with her eyes at the English girl, but looks cannot hurt.

As Lady Ruth utters her last words, she makes a sudden move.

With a dexterous fling of an arm she succeeds in tearing from the Sister's face the cleverly-made thin stage mask that was contrived to conceal the features of one who did a double act.

The professor laughs.

From the crowd that is still gathering various sounds arise, for no one can even give a guess as to the nature of the peculiar trick which is thus being enacted.

As for John Craig, he holds his breath at the stupendous nature of the disclosure, for little as he has dreamed of the fact, he sees before him the well-known features of Pauline Potter.

This queen of the stage has made even another attempt to get John, and might have succeeded only for the opportune coming of his friends.

He backs away from her.

"So, it is you again, wretched girl?" he exclaims, in something of righteous wrath.

She has lost once more, but this is frolic to one of her nature, and she laughs in his face.

"Oh, it's a long road that has no turning, and my chance will yet come! Bah! I snap my fingers at such weak friendship. Good-night, all of you, but not good-by."

Thus she disappears.

Craig feels abashed.

He has almost come to blows with his best friend about this female, and, after all, she turns out to be the plotting Pauline.

"I think I need a guardian," he murmurs, as if rather disgusted with himself.

"From the ugly looks some of these chaps are bending on you, I think ditto," declares Philander, nor are his words without meaning, for the natives scowl dreadfully.

"Lady Ruth, I owe you thanks; but, while we walk to the hotel, tell me how you came to know she was masquerading in that style."

"It is easily told, sir. A mere accident put me in possession of the facts, and, thank Heaven, I am able to build two and two together. You were frank enough, Doctor Craig, to give me certain particulars concerning that creature's plotting, and that confidence has now borne fruit.

"Listen, then. I was in the hotel, in my room. Some freak of fortune placed her in the apartment opposite. Knowing what presumably brought her to Algiers, the desire to have revenge upon you, I entertained a feeling of almost contempt for a woman who could so forget her sex and seek a man who loved her not. If it were I whom you jilted, Doctor Chicago, I would freeze you with scorn."

"Jove! I don't doubt it, Lady Ruth, but please Heaven you will never have the chance," he says, in a half-serious, half-joking way.

"To return to my story, then," she continues, blushing under the ardent look that has accompanied his words, "the queer part of it lies in the fact that a transom over my door was partly open. There was a black paper back of the glass, which gave it the properties of a mirror.

"Over her door was a similar contrivance, and as I sat there in the darkness of my room, pondering over what has happened, my attention was attracted by a flash of light, and, looking up, I saw the interior of her room as plainly as though looking through the door—saw her assume the garb of a Sister—saw her try on that horrible face-mask before a mirror, and realized that the clever actress, Pauline Potter, was about to again undertake some quixotic crusade in the furtherance of her plans.

"Later on, Aunt Gwen came and said we had better go outside to hear the music and see the crowd, so I came, but all the while I had been puzzling my brain wondering what she hoped to accomplish with that clever disguise, nor did the truth break in upon my mind until we discovered her talking to Doctor Chicago. Then I comprehended all."

"And I am again indebted to your clever woman's wit," he says, warmly.

"Who can tell from what dreadful fate I saved you," she laughs; "for this same Pauline seems determined that you shall not remain a merry bachelor all your days."

"So far as that is concerned, I quite agree with Pauline. Where we differ is upon the subject that shall be the cause of my becoming a Benedict. She chooses one person, and I chance to prefer another. That is all, but it is quite enough, as you have seen, Lady Ruth, to create a tempest in a tea-pot."

"Here we are at the hotel," she hastens to say, as if fearing lest he push the subject then and there to a more legitimate conclusion, for she has learned that these Chicago young men generally get there when they start; "and I am not sorry for one. Look around you, doctor!"

This he does for the first time, and is startled to discover that they have been accompanied across the square by at least half a dozen natives, who gaze upon John much as might wolves that were kept from attacking the sheep by the presence of faithful guards.

"They don't seem to bear me any good-will, I declare; but I am bound to prosecute my search in spite of every Arab in Algiers," is the only remark he makes, meeting glance for glance.

They have not yet succeeded in cowing the spirit in John

Craig, though the man has a poor chance who incurs the vindictive race hatred of Mohammedan devotees in their own country.

The others enter also.

Sir Lionel, not a whit abashed by the failure of his grand plan for saving the life of Lady Ruth in the harbor of Malta, still haunts her shadow. He knows John Craig has a strong suspicion of the truth, but having read that young man's character before now, feels quite certain that he will not speak of the subject without positive proof, which he cannot secure.

Besides, the Briton came out of the affair with such hard luck, that there is much sympathy for him. He lives in the hope of retrieving his fallen fortunes.

Thus the little party breaks up, to meet again on the morrow.

John Craig's only hope now of success in his quest lies in the Moor, Ben Taleb. If the spirit so moves him, he can bring him and his mother face to face, but whether this will ever come to pass remains to be seen.

John, ere retiring, catches sight of the faithful Mustapha Cadi, who lounges near-by, and who makes a signal, as he catches his employer's eye, that brings Craig to his side.

"Where does the master sleep?" he asks.

John explains the position of his room, having some curiosity to know why the courier asks.

"Monsieur should be careful about leaving his windows open; Arabs climb well; vines very handy; yataghan make no shout. There is no disgrace in being prepared."

This is too broad to admit of any misinterpretation, and John again makes up his mind to continual watchfulness.

He retires to seek rest, to dream of a strange conglomeration of gray eyes, and black and brown—that he is compelled to choose between the English girl, the Chicago actress, and the Moorish beauty, while death waits to claim him, no matter which one he selects.

St. George Rathborne

CHAPTER XV

THE WRECKED STAGE

John Craig takes all the precautions that the courier mentions, for he does not care to awaken in the night and find a dark-faced fanatic of a Mohammedan in his room, sworn to accomplish his death.

Perhaps his safety is in part due to this; at any rate morning comes and finds him undisturbed.

When he descends from his room he has a vague hope that some word may have come from Ben Taleb.

In this respect he is doomed to disappointment, for there is no letter. So another day of waiting begins. The doctor is determined by nature, and has made up his mind that he will not give up his mission until he has accomplished that which he set out to perform, no matter if he spends weeks in the African city at the foot of the hills known as Sahel.

The others join him by degrees.

Such charming weather; a dozen trips for the day are proposed and rejected. All conclude to wait until after breakfast, when they will be in a condition to discuss the matter and decide just what is best to be done.

John is ready to join them and see the sights, for there is a chance that he may in this way run across the one he seeks, if she be moving about the city on errands of mercy, as becomes her order.

Besides, he places considerable dependence upon the promise of the old Moor.

So he enters into the discussion with assumed vigor, being magnetized now by the blue eyes of Lady Ruth.

They ask the advice of Mustapha Cadi, and he promises to show them many queer sights before the sun sinks behind the hills and the boom of the gun in the fortress announces the close of another day.

Thus, all of them prepare for a day's outing, and Lady Ruth looks quite charming in her jaunty costume, especially suited for such business.

John no longer remembers the dazzling beauty of the Moorish girl who sat at the feet of old Ben Taleb on the preceding night; it could not compare with the vivacious intelligence of an educated girl coming from the countries beyond the seas.

First of all they mount the terraces of Mustapha Superieur and enjoy the magnificent view of the city and harbor. Many modern yachts lie upon the blue waters, side by side with strange vessels peculiar to the Mediterranean, while the incoming steamer from Oran is just entering the harbor.

Upon this ridge above the city lie numerous palatial residences now occupied by French and English families, but which were once owned by the pirate kings of Algiers, whose names may often be found upon the gate post, cut in letters of gold.

From this eyrie they scanned the sea with their glasses, and the appearance of a sail in the dim distance would be the signal for a mad chase to see which piratical felucca could first overhaul the stranger.

Uncle Sam had something to do with breaking up this tremendous pirates' den, and France has since redeemed it.

Thus a considerable portion of the morning is consumed in this pleasant engagement. They take an omnibus now for the Arab village of Birkadeen, in among the hills, where new and novel sights will be looked upon.

Every female they meet arouses John's interest, and he looks sharply at the half-hidden face. The hope he cherishes is always before him, and when Lady Ruth notices his eager actions she understands just what it means, and is as anxious in one way as himself.

One thing annoys the American; this is the persistence with which Sir Lionel keeps up as a member of the little company. He makes himself agreeable all around, and as John has had no proof of the Briton's miserable work in the harbor of Malta, he is wise enough to restrain his feelings and hold his tongue, trusting to some future event to tear off the mask and reveal him in his true colors.

At noon they are in the village, and stop to eat their lunch at an Arab tavern, where they fare pretty well, though John is ready to make a vow never to again touch the native dish of Kuskusu which is set before them.

They see strange things at Birkadeen, and from there continue their journey to other villages, Bermandries, and El-Biar, at each of which Mustapha has something odd to show them that will ever remain a pleasant memory in the future.

It is a day John Craig will never forget for more reasons than one; a day marked with a white stone because of the pleasure he enjoys in the society of this bright English girl whom he has ere now learned to love, and a day that must always remain prominent in his mind because it precedes a night that is the most memorable in all his history.

In more ways than one does Lady Ruth, while always acting as a lady, show that she prefers his society to that of Sir Lionel, and though the British soldier appears unruffled on the surface, he is undoubtedly deeply piqued.

So the hours wear on.

The sun is low in the west, and the ever watchful Mustapha declares it is time they started for the city. They have enjoyed a ride on the ship of the desert, as the camel is called, admired the Arabian steeds, which all the money of an unbeliever or Christian dog could not purchase, and looked upon many strange scenes.

Several times during the afternoon they have been temporarily separated. The baronet appears to have a deep interest in the queer things to be seen in the Arab village, for more than once he lingers behind to ask questions as he explains, in the hope of purchasing some article that has particularly caught his fancy.

John never once suspects that Sir Lionel may have another motive in his actions.

When Mustapha announces that it is time they return, they look around for the vehicle which was to take them back, but strangely enough it does not appear.

As the minutes pass Mustapha grows exceedingly impatient. He has arranged matters to suit their convenience, and this delay is annoying. It does not suit him to return at night.

Just as patience ceases to be a virtue, and the guide has announced his intention of finding some other means of transportation, they discover the omnibus coming into view from beyond the thicket of cactus and aloe.

It has been carrying a load of villagers from their homes to the high hills of Bouzaveah, to the native cemetery which crowns the summit.

Then they suddenly remember that it is Friday, or the Mohammedan Sunday, on which day great throngs repair to the grave-yards and visit the tombs of the *marabouts* or saints, gazing upon some ancient relic which the departed wore in his life-time, and which on account of its disreputable condition no respectable European would touch.

They have the omnibus to themselves, which, of course, pleases them.

John shakes his head dubiously as he enters the vehicle. He has glanced at its condition, and declares they will be lucky indeed to reach Algiers without a break-down.

The driver has been scored by Mustapha for his tardiness, and appears to feel the sting of the reproach, for no sooner are they seated in the old vehicle than he uses his whip with some vim, the horses start away, and they head for the city.

When the road is smooth it is all very good, but after leaving Birkadeen they will strike a rough section that must try the staying powers of the wretched vehicle.

As they whirl through Birkadeen in a cloud of dust, with several mangy curs howling at the heels of the steaming horses, it is just sunset. There is no mosque here with its minaret, from which the *muezzin* chants his call to prayer, but the faithful do not need such a summons, and can be seen here and there prostrating themselves on the ground with faces toward the holy city.

One grows accustomed to such spectacles when traveling in oriental countries where Mohammed is looked upon as the great prophet of Allah, and the novelty inspired by the first sight dies away.

After leaving the Arab village they strike the rough section of the road.

It would be natural to suppose that the driver has by this time gotten over his anger at being chided by Mustapha, and might moderate his pace, out of respect to his antiquated vehicle, if not the safety of those who occupy it.

Not so.

If anything, as darkness steals over the scene, he uses his whip with greater energy, and his voice urges on the sweating horses.

Now they have it surely.

The ruts in the road cause the vehicle to bounce from side to side, and those inside are tossed about much like rubber balls.

St. George Rathborne

At first they are disposed to treat it as a joke, and laugh over the ludicrous situation, but as it increases, their sufferings begin.

The dust is disagreeable, the jolting actually dangerous, as they are shot from one side of the vehicle to the other with tremendous force.

Besides, John is in momentary expectation of the rickety affair breaking down and spilling them all out on the roadway.

Indeed, he is surprised that this accident has been so long delayed.

He shouts to the driver to slacken the pace, but evidently the fellow fails to hear. Then he puts his head out of the window and once more elevates his voice, but the rattle of the plunging vehicle, together with the noise made by the driver himself, as he shouts at his steeds like a crazy Bedouin, combine to deaden all other sounds.

At any rate there is no result.

John has by this time become excited; they are mounting a little elevation, and temporarily their pace is reduced. Once at the top and a long slant lies beyond, down which they must go at lightning speed.

It is now or never.

He is bound to stop this mad race against time if he has to climb to the top of the swaying vehicle and toss the reckless driver off.

It is with this intention before him that he bids the ladies hold on with all their power, while he seeks an interview with the fellow who handles the ribbons.

Then he seizes the window-frame, intending to get hold of something above which will serve as a fulcrum to move his body.

It is just at this interesting moment that the expected event occurs.

There is a sudden, tremendous shock, as they strike some obstacle; shrieks from the women, a swaying of the coach, which immediately falls over on one side.

A wheel has come off.

They are wrecked among the hills, and a considerable distance from Algiers, the lights of which illumine the heavens beyond.

"Is anyone injured?" calls out John, with some anxiety in his voice, for the shock has been quite serious.

They are all in a confused heap in the corner that is down, and the professor is the first to crawl out.

Then comes Lady Ruth, excited, but, thank Heaven, uninjured.

They help Sir Lionel out. He limps around, feeling his left leg and groaning a little as even the bravest of men may do on occasions, and hoping the pain he feels is nothing serious.

Aunt Gwen alone remains, and there is heard no sound from her. The usually vociferous voice seems to have been utterly hushed.

"Oh! is she dead?" exclaims the young girl, with horror in her voice, as Doctor Chicago and the professor carry Aunt Gwen out.

"I trust not. I think she has only fainted. Can you lift one of the cushions from the wreck, Lady Ruth, and we will place her upon it here."

She shows immediate animation instead of going into hysterics, as many girls would do under the circumstances, and flies to assist to the extent of her ability.

Thus Aunt Gwen is soon in a comfortable position, and the doctor starts to bring her to, for he believes she has only swooned.

This he soon accomplishes, and when she is able to declare that she is not in pain, only badly broken up by the shock, he feels that it is time he turned his attention to another quarter.

They are in a bad fix, wrecked several miles from their destination.

Darkness has now set in.

John rises from his knees and takes in the situation. It is evident that something must be done in order that they may be rescued from their unpleasant position.

Where are Mustapha and the driver? Both of them have utterly vanished in the most mysterious manner. Who, then, will mount one of the panting horses and ride back to Birkadeen for succor?

"Let me go?" says Sir Lionel, staggering forward, and clutching an olive tree for support.

John sees his weak state.

"You are not in a condition to go. Stay here and protect the ladies, for it is a lonely place, and there may be wild animals in these woods, who knows?" With which words the young American throws himself on the horse's back and urges the animal along over the road they have traveled, followed by the anxious eyes of Lady Ruth.

St. George Rathborne

CHAPTER XVI

A FRENCH WARRIOR

John digs his heels into the sides of the animal he bestrides, and urges him on with every artifice known to a jockey, and considering the darkness, the rough nature of the road, and the weariness of the beast, he succeeds in getting over the ground at quite a respectable rate.

Thus, meeting no one on the way, he finally bursts upon the village of Birkadeen much after the manner of a thunderbolt from a clear sky, and dashes up to the office of the stage line, which, as may be supposed, is managed by Franks.

A Frenchman has charge, and upon his vision there suddenly bursts a dusty figure, with hair destitute of covering, and clothing awry, a figure that has leaped from a horse bathed in sweat; a figure he imagines has broken loose from some mad-house, yet which upon addressing him shows a wonderful amount of coolness.

"Are you the agent of the stage line?" is the first question fired at him.

"I am Monsieur Constans. I have ze charge of ze elegant equipage line zat you speak of as one stage," returns the Frenchman.

"You remember my passing through here a little while ago, bound for Algiers?"

"*Parbleu!* zat is so. I am astonish. What for are you back on ze horseback, too. *Mon Dieu!* have ze robbers been at it again? Ten souzan fury, and ze *cadi* promise zat we have no more trouble wif zem."

At the mention of the word John experiences a sudden chill, remembering that he has left Lady Ruth and Aunt Gwen upon the loneliest part of the road to Algiers; but becomes somewhat reassured when it also crosses his memory that the gallant professor and the soldier hero of Zulu battles are there to defend them.

"You are mistaken. The miserable vehicle has broken down," he says.

"*Ciel!* is zat all?"

"All! Confound your impudence, and isn't it enough when two ladies are almost killed outright by the accident? All! when we've been rattled about like dry peas in a pod, until there's hardly a square inch of me that doesn't ache. I'll tell you, monsieur, what you are to do, and in a dused hurry, too. Order out another stage and fly to the scene of the wreck without delay."

"Begar! if I only had a vehicle," he groans.

"You shall find one of some sort inside of five minutes and go with me to the scene to rescue my friends, and take them to safety, or you must take the consequences," and in his excitement John glowers upon the dapper Gaul until the latter actually trembles with trepidation.

"Stop! I have zink of something. Zere is one old vehicle in ze shed, laid by for repairs. By careful handling it would do."

"Good! Get horses hitched to it; we must lose no time. To the rescue, Monsieur Constans. Ladies have been hurt; they must be taken to the city as speedily as possible."

The Gaul is excitable by nature, and he catches some of John's surplus enthusiasm, springs to his feet, and is out of the office door like a shot, shouting almost unintelligible orders to the gang of dirty Arabs who have rushed to the scene upon the advent of a Frank entering the village like a young cyclone and riding a horse that from its harness they recognize as belonging to the stage line.

John, finding they make such poor headway, proceeds to lend his assistance, and under his directions the job is finally completed.

An old stage, even worse than the wrecked one, is brought out, and the horse John rode harnessed to it. Then a second animal is secured, and after some difficulty about the harness has been adjusted, they are off.

There is, of course, danger that the same catastrophe will happen to them, but the emergency is great, and John handles the reins himself.

Thus through the darkness they proceed, gradually nearing the scene of the disaster.

The nearer they come the more John's fears arise, though he would find it hard to give good reasons for them, since they rest only upon the words that have been let fall by the dapper little French agent who sits beside him on the box, and holds on for dear life, uttering numerous exclamations, in his explosive way, as they pitch and toss.

A tree looms up. John recognizes it as a mark which just preceded their overthrow. Hence, the wrecked stage must lie just beyond, so he pulls in his horse and tries to pierce the darkness that lies like a pall around.

They have at his suggestion brought a lantern along, but of course this is of little use to them as yet.

"What is that cry up on the hill-side?" asks John, as he hears a peculiar sound.

"Monsieur es worry; he need be. Zat is some rascally jackal or hyena; zey hover around ze villages and do much mischief. I have seen zem myself carry off one sheep."

This is not very pleasant intelligence, but John is now engaged in trying to pierce the gloom, and believes he sees some object that may prove to be the wrecked stage.

He sings out with a hail:

"Ah, there, professor!"

Not a reply; only what seems to be an echo is flung back from the hill-side.

Then John's heart stands still with a sudden fear, as he imagines that some terrible thing has occurred. He raises his voice and calls upon Philander. When there comes no reply to this, he makes use of Sir Lionel's name and bellows it forth until the valley seems to ring with the sound. Still hopeless, for no answer bids him drop his fears.

Now the fact is assured that something serious has happened.

John jumps to the ground, desirous of seeing whether they have actually reached the spot where the wrecked omnibus lies.

He finds it to be true, and in another moment is standing upon the very place where Aunt Gwen reclined at the time of his departure.

There is much room for speculation. Any one of half a dozen things might have happened, for to one who is utterly in the dark, there is no end of possibilities.

What can he do?

One chance there is, that while he, Doctor Chicago, was absent, bent upon his errand of mercy and rescue, Mustapha may have once more appeared upon the scene, and influenced the little party to move on in the direction of the distant city.

He still places implicit confidence in the guide, and has strong hopes, though the absence of the Arab at the time of the accident is utterly unexplainable.

By this time monsieur has descended from his perch, and joins him. In his hand he carries the lantern, ready for use.

"What have you found, *mon ami*?" asks this worthy, as he arrives on the scene.

"Here is the wrecked stage, but my friends have vanished. It puzzles me to know what has become of them."

"No doubt they have gone ahead, fearing that you could not

ze new vehicle obtain. We may soon discover ze truth."

"By going forward, yes; but before we do that, perhaps I can learn something about the direction they took."

"Ah! you will apply ze wonderful science of ze prairie. I have heard of it, begar, and I shall be one very glad to see ze experiment."

He poses in an attitude of expectation, and keeps his eyes fastened upon the other, who has already picked up the lantern and bends over, with the intention of following the trail.

This soon brings him from the ruined stage to the olive tree under which they had laid Aunt Gwen.

Arrived here he utters an exclamation.

"This tells the story. Confusion, indeed."

"What now, monsieur?" echoes the Frenchman.

"See; the tracks are numerous."

"But they would have been had these people moved about a good deal."

"Look again. You will note that they are made by other feet. Many men have been here. What you once suggested—"

"*Mon Dieu!* robbers?" as if appalled.

"That explanation is nearer the mark that anything else."

The prospect is appalling, for these wild robbers of the desert fear neither man nor devil, and when once they retreat to their hiding-places in the mountains, it is next to folly to dream of following them.

John Craig finds himself in a dilemma. To whom can he appeal in this, his hour of trial? Will the authorities do anything for him in case the American or British consul make a demand? Can they accomplish aught? These wild Bedouins of the desert do not come under the jurisdiction of the Dey. His orders would be laughed to scorn, and mounted on their swift Arabian steeds they would mock any effort to chase them.

So John is deeply puzzled, and knows not how to turn. If the Frenchman, usually so bright and witty, cannot suggest something to help him out of this dilemma, he will have to depend upon himself alone; but Monsieur Constans shrugs his shoulders and professes to be all at sea.

Dimly John begins to suspect that this may not have been such an accident after all.

He begins to suspect a plot.

The driver? what of him?

His actions had been strange and almost crazy from the start, and yet John feels sure that if the case were thoroughly investigated it would be found that he was not in the habit of thus running with his loads over the rough part of his trip.

There is something unusual in this, and something that demands investigation. The man's actions were suspicious, to say the least, for just as soon as the break-down occurred he had vanished from view.

Evidently he was in league with some one.

John is furious to think that he left the scene of the disaster.

Why did he not let Sir Lionel go? The baronet seemed to be in earnest in his offer, and under such circumstances—but what nonsense after all, to think that he could do more, when the veteran of three wars was evidently unable to prevail against his foes.

Thus, after summing up, John is compelled to admit with a groan that he knows absolutely nothing about the case, and is in a position to learn little more.

He is a man of action, however, and can not bear to see minutes pass without at least an effort to utilize them.

Can they follow the track?

It is a possible solution of the problem, although it promises to be hard work.

Then, again, he thinks of his companion. How far may the Gaul be trusted? He has known Frenchmen who were brave; he has a good opinion of them as a fighting nation, and yet this individual specimen may not turn out to be a warrior.

With the hope of getting an ally, then, he turns to the subject of his anxiety.

"Monsieur Constans."

"I am here."

"Your words have come true. Arab robbers have, I fear, carried off my friends."

"*Mon Dieu!* it ees sad."

"I am determined to rescue them."

"Bravo! bravo!" clapping his hands with the excitement of the moment.

"One thing worries me."

"Ah! monsieur must be plain."

"It concerns you."

"*Le Diable!* in what way?"

"How far can I depend on you?"

At this the French agent draws his figure up with much pomposity. He slaps one hand upon his inflated chest.

"To ze death, monsieur!"

"Good! Tell me, are you armed?"

"It has been my habit, among zese Arabs, zese negroes, zese ragged Kabyles from ze mountains. I would not trust my life wizout zis."

Then he suddenly flourishes before John's eyes, delighted with the spectacle, a genuine American bull-dog revolver, which, judging from its appearance, is capable of doing considerable execution when held by a determined hand, and guided with a quick eye.

John instantly matches it.

"Hurrah!" he exclaims, with enthusiasm, "we are well matched, Monsieur Constans. Let it be the old story of

Lafayette and Washington."

"It ees glorious! Zey won ze fight. Why should not we, monsieur—"

"My name is Doctor John Craig from Chicago."

"I greet you zen, Monsieur Doctaire. Zis is all new business to me. Tell me what to do, and I am zere."

"Then we'll follow these tracks a little and try to learn something about those who were here, their number, whether mounted or afoot, and the probable direction they took."

"Superb! I am one delighted to serve wiz a man of zat caliber. You meesed ze vocation I zink, Monsieur John, instead of ze doctaire you should be ze general."

John knows it will not pay to stop and talk with Monsieur Constans. A Frenchman is inclined to be voluble, and valuable time may be lost.

So he walks on, bending low in order that the lantern light may be utilized. Thus he follows the tracks some little distance, with the fighting Gaul at his elbow, endeavoring to penetrate the darkness beyond.

It is a peculiar situation, one that causes him to smile. This time he is not tracking the deer through the dense forests of Michigan. Somewhere ahead are fierce Arab foes who have his friends in their hands.

At the same time he has a vague feeling of alarm in the region of his heart, alarm, not for himself, but concerning the fortunes of Lady Ruth.

A month, yes, hardly more than two weeks before, John Craig did not know there was such a being in existence.

Even when first made acquainted with her he had believed her rather haughty, according to his American notion of girls.

Gradually he has come to know her better, has come to understand the piquant character underlying what he was pleased to look upon as pride, and which her aunt must have had in mind when she gave her the significant name of Miss Caprice.

Thus events have rolled on until now, in this period of suspense, when the girl seems to be in desperate danger, he awakens to the fact that he loves her.

With Monsieur Constans at his side, John has gone perhaps a few hundred yards when the light of the lantern suddenly falls upon a human figure advancing; an Arab, too.

John is about to assume an offensive attitude when he recognizes Mustapha Cadi, the guide.

CHAPTER XVII

ON TO THE METIDJA MINE

A startled exclamation at his side causes the young doctor to remember that he has a companion. He whirls around and just in time to avert what might have turned out to be a catastrophe, for Monsieur Constans, seeing the figure of an Arab coming toward them, has no other idea than that it is an enemy.

Perhaps the fiery Gaul is somewhat anxious to try his fire-arms. At any rate, when John so suddenly wheels upon him, monsieur is in the act of covering the advancing figure.

John with a sharp cry knocks his leveled weapon up, and calls out:

"It is a friend; my guide, Mustapha Cadi."

"*Diable!* I am one fool," exclaims the Gaul. "I recognize ze man now, and but for you he would be dead. I shall beg his pardon. It was one grand meestake."

Meanwhile Mustapha has come up.

Doctor John Craig is filled with a new excitement now. In

his eyes the coming of this man means much. It is strange that no suspicion enters his head in connection with Mustapha. Even while he is so certain that the driver of the omnibus is in league with their enemies; that the break down is only a part of the grand scheme to obtain possession of the English girl who can pay a big ransom, he has never once connected the Arab guide with the matter.

This is all the more singular because Mustapha Cadi was on the top of the coach at the time of the wreck, and he disappeared with the driver.

It can only be accounted for by the fact that like most keen men John Craig is in the habit of relying upon his judgment in such matters, and there is something about the face of Mustapha that wins his confidence.

Then, again, there are the events of the preceding night. The courier stood by him like a Spartan hero; yes, he can be trusted.

Thus John meets the guide warmly, and a new hope immediately springs into existence, a hope born of confidence.

"What does all this mean, Mustapha Cadi? See, I have brought the agent of the stage line, but when we arrive at the scene of the wreck we find it deserted. What does it mean? Have my friends fallen into the hands of robbers?"

Mustapha immediately nods his head.

"It is so, monsieur."

"Who are they?"

"Arabs, Kabyles, Moors—all who hate the Franks, yet love

money more. They are under a desperate leader, the Tiger of the Desert."

At this Monsieur Constans utters a low cry.

"He means Bab Azoun, ze terrible gate-way of death."

Mustapha again nods, and John resumes his cross-questioning with a lawyer's tact.

"Were our friends injured?"

"Not seriously. They fight well. The soldier threatens to kill all, but they do not allow him to do it."

"Brave Blunt; he deserves a Victoria cross. But where were you, Mustapha?"

The Arab hangs his face; he looks sheepish.

"I come up just when all was over. They twenty against one. It would be foolish for me to try and fight. I believe I can do better; so I watch, I follow, I learn much."

John cannot restrain his feelings. He seizes the Arab's dusky hand and shakes it with real Chicago ardor.

"Mustapha, you're a jewel. Go on. Where did you go at the time of the accident?"

"Bismallah! I was after him, the cause of it all—him, who entered into this conspiracy—the driver. Monsieur, he ran like a deer through the dark. I thought to grasp him more than once, but each time he turned and let me hug the air. But success at last."

"You got him?"

"He picked up a stone with his foot and stretched his length on the ground. Here was my opportunity. I embraced it. Both were out of breath, but I held him there, pinned to the earth. Great is Allah, and Mohammed is his prophet."

"Did you make him confess?"

"I tried to persuade by silvery speech, but it did not meet with success. Then I turned to muscular force. Monsieur, when Abdul el Jabel saw I was in earnest, he cried out for fear, and swore by all the prophets that if I would let him live he would confess the truth."

"Good, good!" says John, pleased with the business qualities of his guide.

"*Begar!* it ees better zan one play," mutters the French agent.

"So I made the miserable driver confess that he had entered into an arrangement with one of the robbers to upset us between Birkadeen and Al Jezira, so that they could make the capture."

"The villain! he deserved hanging. I hope you executed Arab justice on him then and there."

Mustapha shakes his head.

"Monsieur forgets. I had given my word. An Arab will never break that. But I let him go after a few kicks, which, you see I have learned to give from the Franks. He will not go back. He now becomes an open ally of Bab Azoun, the desert tiger."

"Well—"

"Monsieur, one word more. He could not tell me all, but gave me to understand that Bab Azoun was in the employ of another party, some Frank who loves revenge."

This opens up a new vista. John is visibly agitated by the news.

"I believe I see light; the hand of Pauline Potter is behind it all."

"Monsieur, pardon."

"Well, what is it now?"

"From all he said I was inclined to believe it was a man who bought Bab Azoun."

"Yes, yes; but you see he may have been mistaken. Besides, Blunt fought like a tiger. It does not matter just now. What we want to do is to rescue them all."

"That is right."

"You came upon the scene just as these friends of mine were overpowered. Tell us what next occurred?"

"A move was made. I feared that it would be the end, for Bab Azoun and his followers usually dash into the desert when they have secured plunder, the pursuit from the French soldiers being what they fear, since the Algerian rulers have given all over into the hands of the Franks.

"Monsieur, I was surprised to see them start off on foot. I was more than pleased to find that they took a *chemin de travers* or what you call a country cross road that leads to the deserted mines or caves of Metidja. This told me they were encamped there, and I heard one man telling another they would not leave until morning, as they had other business in hand."

At this John plucks up courage. The thought of Lady Ruth being miles away, mounted on a fast horse and speeding toward some desert fastness of the robbers, was one to almost paralyze his brain, for the chances of his doing anything to help her in such a case were few and far between.

"What can we do, Mustapha? We are bold and determined, still we are only three against an army. The odds are great."

"Ah! monsieur, it might be beyond our power to overcome the fighters of Bab Azoun by force, but there are other ways."

"Thank Heaven, yes."

"The battle is not always to the strong, nor the race to the swift."

"He speaks like ze prophet," murmurs Monsieur Constans, gazing upon the sublime face and magnificent figure of the Arab courier with something that partakes of the nature of awe.

"True, we are three—they are forty. If we venture to attack we will meet death. That is very good; death comes to all men, and the Koran teaches us that the brave who die in battle, with their faces toward the foe, are transported imme-diately to paradise. That is why the followers of Mohammed never know fear in a battle. But if we die, what then becomes of those in the hands of Bab Azoun?"

"Ay, what indeed?" mournfully.

"Therefore, to save them, monsieur, we must try to live."

"It ees good; we will live," echoes the Gaul.

"And rescue the prisoners of the desert tiger."

"How far away are these deserted mines?"

"About a mile."

"Among the hills on this side of the plain known as Metidja?"

"It is even so, illustrious Frank, on a line with that snowy peak, Djara Djura, which towers above the Atlas Mountains."

"Your plan, Mustapha—speak, for I know you have been considering it."

The courier places his hand on his chest and bows. Praise delights even the tympanum of an Arab, and flattery gains favors in the most unexpected quarter.

"*Ciel!* we are in the agony of suspense," declares the Frenchman, never once taking his eyes off the Arab's face.

"Great is Allah, and Mohammed is his prophet. I am but as a grain of sand on the sea-shore. Let the praise be his."

With this preliminary, Mustapha Cadi gives his plan of action briefly.

It was his intention to go to Al Jezira, to seek the French commandant at the barracks known as the Kasbah, and give him the information concerning Bab Azoun.

It has long been the ambition of the various French generals stationed in Algeria to kill or capture the notorious desert prince who for years has defied their power, suddenly making a bold dash upon some point, and, leaving smoking ruins in his wake, as mysteriously vanish.

Again and again have they sought to track his band over the plains, along the desert and into the wild recesses of the mountains, but it has always turned out a failure. Bab Azoun, on his native heath, laughs them to scorn, and once laid an ambuscade in which the soldiers suffered badly.

Hence, it can be set down as certain that the military governor of Algiers will be delighted with a chance to surround the tiger of the desert, and his band, so close to the city—that as soon as the news is carried to him he will fit out a secret expedition against the enemy.

Now that there are three of them instead of one, it is not necessary that all should go. A single messenger is enough.

Whom shall it be?

Fate decrees.

They look to Monsieur Constans. Mustapha is needed to serve as a guide to the old mines, and Doctor Chicago ought to be on hand, because it is to rescue his friends they go.

Even the French agent recognizes this fact.

"*Parbleu!* Monsieur Craig, it ees right I should go. Besides, I am well acquaint wiz ze commandant. Zen let us consider ze business as settle. I sall away to ze Kasbah, and zen in due time look for ze swoop of ze French zouaves. *Begar!* if Emile Constans may have a hand in ze capture of zat deevil, ze reward will allow him to visit ze adorable Paris again. I am off. I sall let nothing stop me. *Allons!*"

With a majestic wave of the hand he turns his back on them and runs.

They stand and listen.

Plainly can they hear him plunging on through the darkness in the direction of the spot where the old stage was left. Once, twice he measures his length on the ground, only to scramble to his feet, and uttering choice Parisian invectives, continue his flight.

"Now he reaches the stage," says John.

Then comes the crack of a whip.

"They are off. Jupiter! what a noise he makes! How the old stage rattles and bangs. The man is raving mad to plunge over such ground at a reckless pace like that. He will surely meet the same fate, sooner or later, that befell the old vehicle we were in. He only thinks of the reward; of a great holiday lasting six months, on the boulevards and in the cafes of Paris. Sometimes there's a slip between—Great Scott! he's over!" as there comes a grand smash and then utter silence.

Mustapha appears uneasy.

"Monsieur, it is their worst fault; they are too hot-blooded. Not so the English. He is dead."

"Hark!"

Now they hear the clatter of a horse's hoofs; the sound heads toward Algiers.

"Has that horse a rider, Mustapha?" asks John, ready to rest his decision upon the trained ear of the Arab.

"It is even so. You hear yourself; he runs too regularly to be loose."

As he speaks they catch a cry from the quarter where the horse runs, a cry as of a rider urging his steed on.

"That is enough. Monsieur Constans is on the way to the Kasbah. Now we can turn our heads in the direction of the mines of Metidja."

"It is well. Follow me, monsieur," says the courier, gravely.

"We may need this," holding up the lantern.

"It would be dangerous to carry it, for the eyes of Bab Azoun's men are like owls'. Besides, monsieur, we do not need it. Another lantern will give us all the light Allah desires."

As he speaks he points toward the east, where, just peeping above the hill-top, is a golden rim like a monster eye that is about to be fastened upon the earth below.

"The moon; that is a blessing. I accept it as an augury of success. Mustapha, I am ready. Lead on, and may the God of battles decide for the right."

CHAPTER XVIII

THE MODERN LEONIDAS

Mustapha Cadi, like most Arabs, possesses many of the properties that in times gone by distinguished our American Indians.

The signs of the desert and mountains are like an open book to him, and he is quite at home in an undertaking of this sort, a mission requiring energy and daring, as well as caution.

So, without much apparent trouble, he leads the young Chicagoan along. Sometimes the way is difficult, indeed, impossible in John's eyes, but the Arab knows the secret, and finds a passage where none appears to exist.

Thus they advance for nearly an hour. John imagines they have gone farther than is the case. This is on account of the rough ground.

"Now, caution. We draw near the place. They will be on the watch. Monsieur knows what discovery means."

"Yes—death. That is understood, but it does not prevent me from desiring to advance. Still we will redouble our caution."

They see lights. These appear to come from openings in the hill, doubtless mouths of the deserted mines, which the robber band of Bab Azoun occupy temporarily, with their accustomed boldness.

Drawing still nearer, under Mustapha's clever guidance, they discover that the main body of the robbers are encamped in the largest cavern, and as it seems natural that they would bring their prisoners here, the two men devote their time toward looking up that quarter.

The Arab courier has played as a boy in these old mines, and knows all about them. This knowledge may serve him well now, and John is pleased to think he is in the hands of one so well informed.

In half an hour they have managed to learn an important fact. The prisoners are in the main cavern. All escape is cut off by the presence of numerous guards at the mouth of the mine, and they are watched besides.

Mustapha, putting his knowledge of the place into good use, has led his companion into a cleft where there is hardly room to crawl; but, as they reach the end, they have a chance to gaze upon the interior where the Arabs and Kabyles, the Moors and negroes, who battle under the free banner of Bab Azoun, are assembled.

Eagerly John looks upon the face of Lady Ruth. His heart seems in his throat, and he no longer can deceive himself regarding his true feelings toward this young lady.

"What can we do?" he whispers to the Arab.

"Nothing but wait," is the reply.

John has a great fear tugging at his heart. On their way they have discussed the situation, and Mustapha has related the habits of the Arab desert outlaws. Should it appear that a rescue was imminent, it was their habit to murder any prisoners.

Surely this is enough to arouse John's keenest fears. What if the French forces do come and annihilate the robber host—if the prisoners share their doom, what has been gained?

That is why he asks so anxiously if there is nothing to be done.

The Arab by this time realizes why he is so anxious, and hesitates a little before making reply.

"We must watch and wait. Monsieur will see something soon. Watch the soldier."

This gives John a new idea, and he speedily discovers that Sir Lionel is not idle. The soldier has been in too many desperate situations to be dismayed over such a trifling thing as this.

He is not bound, and hence can move about. Now he seems to be talking to the professor, and anon with Aunt Gwen. Last of all he speaks to Lady Ruth, who nods eagerly.

And a strange feeling comes up in John's mind as he surveys this scene. What causes him to remember the harbor of Malta, the words of the boatman before leaving the steamer, the tragic scene in the blue waters?

It comes over him like a flash. Perhaps he did Sir Lionel an injustice when he suspected him of criminal plotting in such a case, but the circumstances were decidedly against the man.

If he could be guilty of such a scheme, what would he not do in order to win favor at the hands of the young English beauty?

Again it flashes through John's mind; did not the driver in speaking of the facts tell Mustapha that in his opinion it was a man who had entered into a conspiracy with Bab Azoun?

John's first thought was of Pauline Potter—that she had hoped to get hold of him; but now he changes his mind, and locates the trouble elsewhere, fixing it upon the veteran.

Under these circumstances it may be interesting to see how the Briton intends working his plan. John's only desire is a sincere wish that Lady Ruth may be rescued from her predicament. He has no wish to put her to any unnecessary trouble in order that he may play the hero. As well Sir Lionel as any one else, so long as she is benefited.

With this spirit, he can watch the development of affairs composedly, though the suspicion that has crept into his mind causes him a little worry.

Sir Lionel is evidently getting ready to make a move for liberty. His very actions betray it in more ways than one. John cannot but think that he goes about it with something like a flourish of trumpets that is hardly in keeping with the situation, for it is supposed that a dozen pairs of eyes are upon them.

First of all, he secures a weapon that is hanging upon the wall near-by. It must be his own revolver, John believes. How lucky that the Arabs hung it so close to his hand. No one appears to notice the action. Really, Sir Lionel is attended by the goddess of luck.

Then the professor makes a move in the same direction, crawls forward, and lays hands on a gun that rests against the wall. This he smuggles back with him, and again the guards are all interested in other business, laughing, and joking.

So far, good. Perhaps they can, if this marvelous good fortune follows them, steal all the arms in the camp, and even capture the brigade. So John concludes with a smile, as he sees what the professor has done.

Anxiously, he waits to see what there will be next on the programme. Some of the guards have left the place, others lie down to sleep.

"The grand climax is coming," he thinks, as he takes note of these things. "Blunt is getting ready to sweep the board. Well, good luck to him."

Even Mustapha has discovered that something strange is on the *tapis*.

He has a singular way of expressing it.

"Poor Monsieur Constans," he whispers.

"What is the matter with him?" ejaculates John, in about the same tone.

"It is too bad."

"Mustapha, speak out."

"He will come after a while."

"Yes, yes."

"And he will find no Bab Azoun, no band of illustrious robbers to do battle with."

John's mind instantly hits upon flight as the cause for all this.

"Why do you speak so?"

"This wonderful soldier, he do it all; by the mighty power of his arm he will overcome the hosts of Bab Azoun. Great is Allah, and Mohammed is his prophet; but I have never seen such a thing before in all my life."

Then the exquisite, dry humor of the thing strikes John, and with such force that he comes very near bursting with laughter.

He has not the slightest desire to do anything that will bring about a change in the plan. So long as Lady Ruth is rescued from her unpleasant position, it matters little what the means are.

Hence, he watches the development of matters with a keen interest. It is not long before he is in a position to see that there is solid truth in his suspicions. The actions of Sir Lionel confirm the fact that he has been induced to compromise his honor in order to succeed with John as a rival.

When the divine spark touches the heart, it causes men to do strange things.

Here is one who in times past has been very jealous of his honor, and would as soon cut off his hand as compromise himself. Yet, reduced to sore straits by the success of a rival, he now descends the scale, and schemes as cleverly as any rascally adventurer.

The critical period draws near, and our military hero can scarce restrain his valor. Indeed, he shows symptoms of wanting to rush out and annihilate the whole band of Arabs and Moors, but Lady Ruth restrains him, as though she is clever enough to see the folly of a move too premature.

It is a picturesque scene, and one that John will never forget. The grotto alone has charming features, since the walls are white and incrusted with some metallic substance that shines like silver.

On either side can be seen giant stalactites dependant from the roof, looking like mighty columns to support the dome.

The fire and the torches illumine the scene, until it looks like one of enchantment. The strange costumes of the nomads, with the various colors they boast, add to the romantic nature of the exposition, and his must be a poor soul, indeed, that fails to catch something of artistic fervor when such a picture appears in view.

There were twenty of Bab Azoun's men present an hour before, but now only half of that number can be seen.

The remainder have mysteriously disappeared. Things seem to be working to suit the desperate plans of the veteran Zulu fighter, and he will soon be in a condition to open the engagement.

There will doubtless be a battle. John is lost in admiration of the genius that could prepare such a scene, such a triumph. He does not anticipate that even if the Briton is successful in his plans, he will carry the heart of Lady Ruth by storm.

"We must move," whispers Mustapha.

St. George Rathborne

"Why?" asks John, desiring enlightenment.

"So as to be ready to take a hand in the grand affair," is the reply.

Up to this moment it has not occurred to the young man from Chicago that he may be in a position to profit by this peculiar situation.

He smiles with the idea.

"Mustapha, I leave all in your hands. Do with me as you please."

"Then come."

They quit the cleft, using great caution to prevent discovery. The plans of the Arabian guide are soon made manifest, for he signifies his intention of securing a sentry who paces up and down outside the old mine.

If he were a baby he could not have made less resistance. John would have been amazed only that he has been forewarned. It is not the guard's policy to attempt an outcry— undoubtedly he has had his orders.

"Well?" says Mustapha, after the fellow has been tied up, and prevented from making an outcry.

"I believe we can capture the whole outfit at that rate. I feel equal to twenty myself. They must have taken some drug; they have no more life than a mummy from the pyramids."

The Arab grins as though he enjoys the joke.

"It is coming, prepare to see the mighty Frank's wonderful work."

Even as he speaks, they hear loud shouts within the old mine —shouts that would indicate an upheaval—shouts from Arab lips, that echo from the Kabyle throats.

They seem to indicate astonishment—fear.

Above them rises the bellow of a Briton, rushing to the fray with the eagerness of an infuriated bull.

Oh, it is grand!—it is beautiful to see that one man hurl himself on half a dozen! Fear—he knows not the meaning of the word it seems—his opponents monopolize that.

John, looking in, is delighted with the spectacle, and laughs to himself as he sees how remarkably deadly are all Sir Lionel's shots. A man falls every time he pulls trigger; if he rushes at a fellow, so great is the fear his awful presence inspires that the wretched Arab sinks down and actually expires through fright.

The doctor has seen some wonderful stage fights, but the equal of this, never. He laughs, yet finds himself almost stupefied with amazement. Truly, the Victoria cross would well become this remarkable hero.

One or two of the dead men do not seem to have had enough, or else are dissatisfied with the manner of their taking off. At any rate, they stagger to their feet, and have to be put to sleep again by energetic means.

Philander comes near making a mess of it all by his enthusiasm. It is a regular picnic to the small professor.

St. George Rathborne

In the beginning he aimed his gun at one of the brigands. The weapon is strange to him, being a long Arabian affair, with a peculiar stock, but Philander has some knowledge of weapons, shuts his eyes, and pulls the trigger.

The report staggers him. When he opens his eyes, and sees the big, ragged Kabyle at whom he aimed lying flat on his back, with arms extended, the professor is horrified at first.

Then some of the warlike spirit that distinguished his ancestors at Lexington begins to flame up within him.

He gives a shrill war-cry that would doubtless please many a Greek scholar, and plunges headlong for the foe.

The way in which he swings that Arab gun is a sight to behold; in itself the apparition of Professor Sharpe thus advancing to the fray is enough to strike terror to the human heart.

One poor devil is in a position to receive a tremendous whack on the back with the gun, now used as a cudgel, and there is positively no fraud about the manner of his sprawling around.

After that the professor sweeps the air in vain with his weapon. Men who have met the terrors of the Algerian desert for years, fall down and expire before he can hasten their exit from this vale of tears.

Really, it is wonderful—he never before knew the tenets of the Mohammedan religion made its devotees so accommodating; they seem to court dissolution in the longing for paradise, where the prophet promises eternal happiness for all who die in battle.

It ends; even such obliging fellows as these do not need to be killed more than a couple of times. Lady Ruth had covered her eyes with her hands when the action began.

She is the daughter of a soldier race, and as brave as the majority of her sex; still she shudders to gaze upon the taking of human life.

Perhaps, too, she anticipates the death of the valorous Briton, who has hurled himself so impetuously into the breach, for under all ordinary conditions his chances would seem to be small.

When the dreadful racket is over, when the shouts, shrieks, and report of fire-arms die away, Lady Ruth uncovers her eyes.

She fully expects to see a slaughter-pen, with the valorous Sir Lionel and Philander among the slain. As to the latter, there are no lack of them, for they lie in every direction, and in every position the human mind can conceive.

And here is the hero warrior rushing up to her, a smoking revolver in one hand. His usual coolness and *sang froid* are gone—Sir Lionel is actually excited. It is not every day that even a veteran of the Cape wars is given a chance to thus immortalize himself after the manner of Samson.

"My dear Lady Ruth, the way is clear. We must fly before the rest of the rascals appear. Perhaps we may be fortunate enough to find horses outside, then a hot dash and the city will be gained. Permit me to assist you."

The girl springs up, ready to accept the chance a kind fate has thrown in her way, and with a startled, curious glance at the piles of slain that incumber the cavern, follows her friends.

St. George Rathborne

CHAPTER XIX

WAR—HORRID WAR!

These strange events have occurred with great rapidity, and yet, of course, they have taken some little time.

It would seem as though the remainder of Bab Azoun's band, if anywhere in the vicinity, might by this time have arrived on the spot, but they do not show up, which fact is a fortunate one for them, though it takes away from the luster of Sir Lionel's fame.

When the four fugitives come out of the old mine into the moonlight, the soldier looks about him quickly.

"If we could only find horses," he cries.

"What's this?" asks Philander.

A whinny sounds close by.

"This way, friends. Bless me! if this isn't the acme of good luck! Here are horses—three, four of them, just one apiece, by Jove!"

"Oh, how singular! I mean how fortunate!" exclaims

Lady Ruth.

There are the animals, fastened to branches of the trees. Why they are separated from the remainder of the herd is not explained.

Sir Lionel never looks a gift of fortune in the face, but when his eyes fall upon the four miserable worn-out hacks which have thus fallen to their share, he grits his teeth, and Philander is puzzled to understand what he just catches:

"Duse take the bloody heathen! A hundred pounds and four such scarecrows!"

Perhaps he is thinking of the chances of their being over-hauled by the men of Bab Azoun, mounted on swift coursers, for there are none who ride better than these desert warriors, and none who own such steeds.

"Let us mount—seconds are precious. There, by throwing one stirrup over, it will make a fair lady's saddle. Allow me, Lady Ruth."

They are speedily mounted. Aunt Gwen seems quite at home on a horse, which she has ridden many times in the Blue Grass regions of Kentucky. As to Philander, the same does not apply. He acts as though in deadly fear of being pitched over the animal's head. The fates decree that the largest horse of all falls to his lot, a raw-boned, loose-jointed specimen of equine growth, and the little professor looks like a monkey perched aloft.

If the beast ever had any martial ardor, it has long ago died out, and yet to the excited fancy of the professor, he might as well be upon the back of a prancing, rearing, snorting war-horse. When the equine wonder shakes his long ears,

Philander imagines he is about to perform some amazing trick, and, filled with a new dread, he clasps his arms around the poor creature's neck, and calls out:

"Whoa! there's a good fellow—be quiet now! I wouldn't hurt you, boy! Whoa! I say. Hang me if I don't believe you've got the devil in you. Want to kill me, eh? No, you don't. Easy now, you rascal. Whoa, whoa!"

Fortunately for Philander the horse follows the lead of the others, and the professor is not left behind.

All seems working well.

Sir Lionel, the undaunted veteran, can afford to smile. Success is apparently assured, for they have gone some little distance, and only now do the clamorous sounds from their rear indicate a commotion.

Pursuit may be made, but it will be useless, as they are not many miles from the walls of Algiers, which will give them shelter.

It looks like a big success, and surely after the wonderful events of this night Lady Ruth cannot ignore the claims he presents. She must fall into the arms of the hero who has rescued her from the Arab host.

So probably he reasons.

But fate hits the man of valor a cruel blow, and that just when it seems as though he has success between his fingers.

It happens naturally enough. At the time a portion of Bab Azoun's piratical band chanced to be separated from the main body, and were under orders to join them at the

Metidja mines.

Coming up the slope, they are amazed to see a little band of pilgrims advancing, lashing their plugs of horses desperately, in the hope of making good time.

The fatal moonlight betrays the fact that this little party is made up of the hated Franks, and hearing the tremendous commotion that has now arisen in the direction of the cavern, it is easy to line up the case, and conclude that the party has escaped.

Hence it is that all of a sudden Sir Lionel finds himself in the midst of half a dozen Arab riders, who bar farther progress.

It is the unexpected that happens.

He attempts the same system of tactics that were so successful in the previous difficulty, but they do not pass current with these fierce men.

Immediately the two Franks are set upon by the desert tigers. Two seize Sir Lionel and drag him from his steed, he resisting desperately. What a great pity he exhausted his resources so thoroughly in the first round. Ten men could not overcome him then, while two manage to hold him quiet now.

Philander, emboldened by his former success, thinks he can show them a trick or two that will count; but a blow chances to fall upon his bony steed's haunches, starting the animal off, and the professor, throwing valor to the four winds, proceeds to clasp his arms tightly around the horse's neck, shouting out an entreaty for some one, in the name of Julius Cesar, Mohammed, or Tom Jones, to stop the wicked beast before he makes mince-meat of his master.

St. George Rathborne

One of the desert raiders gallops alongside, and, clutching the bridle, turns the runaway around.

By this time the commotion above has increased, and it even sounds as though the men of Bab Azoun might be starting out in quest of the fugitives who have given them the slip.

What are these sounds closer by—the thunder of many hoofs, the wild neighing of steeds? It is as though a squad of French cavalry might be rushing down upon them.

The leader of the small Arab force gives quick orders, and his men immediately fall into line of battle, ready to meet the foe, if perchance such proves to be the character of the cavalcade.

Now they burst out of the aloe thicket—they come dashing straight on toward the spot where the little company is gathered.

The moonlight falls upon them. Most of the horses are seen to be riderless, yet they are the pet steeds of the outlaws, animals upon the backs of which they have committed depredations on the desert, and laughed pursuit to scorn.

Upon two of the foremost chargers human figures may be seen, and one glance tells them who these worthies are.

Lady Ruth is the first to exclaim:

"Why, it is John Craig."

"He will be killed, see these fellows getting ready to fire. John, take care!" and Aunt Gwen, in her eager desire to warn the doctor, waves her hands in the air, one of them grasping a fluttering white kerchief.

They hear the cry, they see the signal, and their eyes take in the line of dusky warriors that awaits their coming.

"Down, monsieur!" exclaims Mustapha.

Not a second too soon do they drop upon the necks of their horses, for a blinding flash comes from the men of Bab Azoun, a flash that is accompanied by a roar, and a hail-storm of lead sweeps through the space occupied by the forms of John Craig and his guide just a brief interval before.

"Charge!" cries Craig, rising in his seat, his face white with the strange battle spirit, his right hand clutching a weapon.

Then comes a scene of action that is totally unlike the one preceding it, for now both sides are in deadly earnest, and the battle is a royal one, indeed.

When Craig fires he aims to diminish the number of his foes. Sometimes a rearing horse gets the benefit of the flying lead.

For the space of a minute or so the utmost confusion reigns. At first the string of horses that the bold Craig and his guide were running away with, becomes a feature in the scene, prancing and shrilly neighing. Then they break and scatter in many directions.

There were six Arabs originally in the party, but Philander knocked one *hors de combat* with the tremendous whack of a gun he snatched from its keeper.

Another drops from his horse before the fire of Doctor Chicago, and Mustapha, who handles a yataghan with mar-velous dexterity, actually cleaves a third to the chin with the keen blade.

There is a brief but exceedingly lively engagement between the survivors and the Franks; but the tide of battle is with the strangers in Algiers.

Wounded and fairly beaten, the three raiders at last whirl their horses and dash madly away. Perhaps they are wise. It sometimes takes Sir Lionel a little while to get in motion, but that great fire-eater is about ready to enter the engagement at the time they fly, thus showing rare wisdom.

The field is won.

John hears the shouts of the pursuers close by, while sharp whistles sound, signals which are meant for the stray horses, loose from the kraal, which they are bound to obey.

"We must make use of every second. They will be after us," he says, hastily.

Lady Ruth shudders when she sees one of the Arabs endeavoring to stanch a wound in his shoulder. There is no mimic war here, it is evident.

When they start in a little squad, it is with a faint hope of making such progress that the enemy must give up the pursuit; but almost immediately John discovers something that gives him uneasiness.

His horse staggers. It is evident that the beast has been struck with a flying piece of lead, and is about to fall under him.

The doctor says nothing, and hopes his absence may not be noticed by the flying column, but, as it happens, when the catastrophe does occur, all of them see it.

Fortunately John clears himself just in time, and reaches the ground in safety. Lady Ruth pulls in her horse.

"You must not stop!" cries John; "urge your horses on—fly while you have time. I hear them coming!"

He tries to start Lady Ruth's nag, but she pulls on the lines.

"I decline to run and leave you here, Doctor Chicago," she says, resolutely.

"But you must go," he declares.

"Nonsense!" breaks in Philander. "Here's room for you, John. Jump up."

The young man sees that the quickest way to get them started is to obey, so he manages to reach the saddle in front of the professor, who clasps his arms about him and holds on.

This done, they clatter on again.

It soon becomes evident that their pursuers gain upon them rapidly, despite their best efforts. There can be but one end to the race, and this is in plain view.

John keeps his wits about him. If caught upon the open by the rushing column of fierce desert warriors, a desperate engagement must ensue, which will doubtless end in their complete annihilation, for it can hardly be expected that Sir Lionel will be able to play his great game twice on the same night.

The Englishman has maintained a stolid silence all this while. Perhaps he is out of humor at the change in the arrangements, and fears lest, after all his hard work, the young Chicagoan may carry off the palm.

　　　　　　　St. George Rathborne

Past experience has been of that order.

Hence he moves without much animation. There seems to be a fatality about the sudden appearance of Doctor Chicago on the scene.

Meanwhile John Craig is not bothering his head about the small side-issues connected with the matter, which will work out their own final adjustment. He is more concerned regarding their escape from the threatening doom that seems ready to ingulf them.

Something must be done, that is certain, beyond all peradventure, and John quickly grasps the situation. There is no disease that does not have its remedy, and he finds a loop-hole of escape here.

As they gallop along they come to a structure built upon the road-side—a singular affair it was once upon a time, being made of stone. John recognizes features that tell him this deserted place was once a holy spot, the tomb of a *marabout*, or saint, built in a manner to suit the taste of the departed.

It has been long deserted, as too public, and the holy relics moved to some more secluded tomb within the walls of the cemetery on the high hill of Bouzareah.

This is their chance.

To continue the race means positive overhauling and doubtless death, while by accepting the chance that fortune has thrown in their way they may keep their enemies at bay until aid comes, for John has not forgotten the mission of Monsieur Constans.

He calls a halt, and briefly explains his plans. All of them see that the horses they ride are not in the race when compared with the magnificent steeds of their pursuers, and recognizing the fact that what John suggests is probably the best thing to be done under the existing circumstances, they quickly dismount.

The horses are then started along the road in the hope that they will lure the pursuers on while the little party pass through the opening, and enter the quaint building, once the resting-place of a holy Mohammedan's bones.

CHAPTER XX

THE COMING OF THE FRENCH ZOUAVES

Perhaps Mustapha Cadi, as a true Mohammedan, may have a certain amount of respect for this odd tomb of a *marabout*, but, as the saint's bones have been removed, he has no hesitation about making a fort out of the rocky recess.

When all have entered he closes the opening. The door is broken, but there are many loose stones around that can be made to serve.

There is no time just now to use them, for the rush of horses' hoofs are heard up the road, as the men of Bab Azoun come racing along, intent upon overhauling the fugitives.

They sweep past the rocky tomb like a young cyclone; it is a spectacle none of those who gaze upon it will ever forget. The moonlight renders it perfectly plain, and they can even see the savage expression of each Arab face as the riders dash by.

Now they are gone, and Mustapha begins to pile up the rocks against the door.

The others see what he is about, and immediately assist him, so that when a couple of minutes have elapsed they have made use of every available stone, and can regard their work with considerable satisfaction.

The roof of the tomb is the worst part, and, being made of wood, it shows signs of decay. They locate themselves as best the circumstances will allow and await the sequel.

It is too much to hope that their enemies will long be deceived by the trick that has been played. When they overtake, or sight, the riderless horses, they must grasp the situation, and whirling about, look for the fugitives upon the back trail. No doubt their shrewdness will at once tell them just where those they seek may be found.

Even as they finish their labor and take their positions, those in the tomb discover that a change has come; the shouts of the robbers are growing, louder, showing that they no longer race away. Their tenor has changed, too, and they sound vindictive in their anticipated triumph.

"Ready! they come!" remarks the sententious guide, who takes matters in a cool manner, showing no sign of emotion.

There can be no mistaking the fact, for in another minute the angry band is in front of the old tomb.

Then begins a scene that savors of horrid war. The clamor of battle is in the air, loud shouts ring out, men charge, shots are fired, and with serious result.

Those who defend the fort know their lives are at stake, and they endeavor to make each shot tell. Even Sir Lionel has managed to reload his revolver, and this time makes sure that it contains lead.

The professor is bound not to be left, and as he has secured the long gun which was fastened to the saddle of the bony steed he rode, he sends its contents among the assailants, even as they make their rush.

The result is disastrous to Philander, since it knocks him off his perch; but, scrambling to his feet again, he looks out in time to see that his shot has played havoc among the animals of the attacking force. Three are down, and their riders crawl from underneath, doubtless pretty well scared, if not seriously injured.

The first assault is over—the result is disastrous to the Arabs, who have received severe wounds among them.

They will probably reason the thing over now, and proceed upon new lines, which will possibly bring them nearer success than they have been thus far.

Our friends are not over-confident, even though they have won the first round. They know the tenacious character of the foe against whom they are pitted, and feel sure this is only the beginning. What the end may be only Heaven knows.

The breathing spell is occupied by them in reloading. Lady Ruth and Aunt Gwen arise to the occasion, and beg to be allowed to do anything that falls in their line. If there was only a spare weapon, the English girl declares she could easily load it, but it happens they have none.

Once more breaks out the noise of battle. Whatever may have been the original plans of Bab Azoun and his men, they have long since been forgotten. Revenge is the leading fact in their minds now, revenge for what has been done on this night.

An Arab is a good hater, especially if the object of his animosity be a Christian dog, an unbeliever. Nothing can be too cruel to inflict upon such a foe.

Those within the tomb have aroused the worst passions of the robbers, and can look for no mercy.

The engagement is bitter, indeed, for the Arabs have separated, and creep upon the place on all sides. They discover the weakness of the roof, and bend their energies toward crushing this in.

There is a hot scene, and more than one of the sailants feel the breath of flying lead, together with the sudden sting that tells of a burning wound.

It would be hard to say how the affair might have terminated were the original combatants allowed to carry it to a conclusion, for both sides are desperate, and one of them would have to win.

John has not been without hope. He believes the French zouaves from the Kasbah must long ere this have started on their secret march toward the old mines of Metidja, and he feels sure the noise of battle must direct them to the spot where the fierce engagement is in progress.

Men will fight like tigers when all they have in the world is at stake. John is nerved to greater deeds of valor by the fact that Lady Ruth is present. He shudders at the thought of her falling into the hands of these wild desert rovers.

Finding their efforts to beat in the door useless, the assailants turn their whole attention toward the roof. Great stones are hurled upon it, and the chances of its holding out are few indeed.

When an opening is made a dark face appears at it, and the fellow attempts to push his gun in so that he may fire. Before he can succeed, Mustapha Cadi has leaped upward, and fastened his hand upon the man's throat, and by the weight of his body pulls the fellow through.

Philander snatches up the gun with a cry of delight. He seems to have a weakness for these Arab weapons, on this night, at least, three having passed through his hands. There is heard the sound of a desperate tussle, as the faithful guide battles with his victim.

Again the hole above is darkened, as a human figure attempts to push through, but the British soldier is ready this time. He has the gun Philander threw aside as useless, and, with all his power, he dashes this against the human wedge that fills the opening, sending the fellow whirling over to the ground, shrieking out Arabic imprecations, and calling upon Allah to give the unbelieving dogs into their hands.

More stones are served. They begin to drop through, and it looks serious for those who crouch within. Certainly they cannot hold out much longer.

Heaven is kind, Heaven is merciful. The silent prayers of the two women who kneel within the old tomb are heard.

Just when the clamor of battle is at its height, when the climax is near at hand, they hear a sound that brings joy to the little band, struggling against unequal numbers—a sound that has many times been heard upon the great war-fields of the world—the clear notes of a bugle.

Then come fierce shouts, the cheers of charging zouaves. It is a thrilling period to those who have been almost at the last gasp. Louis Napoleon, struggling at Sedan, could not have heard the zouave battle-cry with more complete satisfaction than they do now.

The Arabs are caught in the very trap they have so long eluded, and it looks like a bad job for them. As to our friends, they are no longer in the affair, and proceed to remove the stones from the door, in order that they may look upon the last scene of the tragic drama.

When this has been done, they see a spectacle that is more pleasing to their eyes than any recently enacted—a scene made up of struggling Arabs and French zouaves, where the latter are five to one—where flashing bayonets meet the cruel yataghan, and the dark deeds of many past years are avenged by the brave soldiers of France.

It is quickly over.

Bab Azoun and his desperate followers expect no mercy, and the French give none. The few Arabs who are uninjured, make a determined assault in one quarter, and literally hew their way through, leaving half of their number on the field.

Few indeed are they who escape, but the victory is shorn of its principal feature, when the fact is disclosed that the dread terror of the desert, the notorious rebel, Bab Azoun, is not among the slain.

He was seen to fall, and yet they cannot find his body, search as they may.

Not being mounted, the French soldiers are unable to give pursuit to the little band that hewed a way out. Besides, they have plenty to do attending to the wounded.

Up to the now open door of the *marabout's* tomb rushes a

figure that has leaped from a horse.

"*Mon Dieu!* tell me, are you safe, ze ladies also?" gasps this party.

It is Monsieur Constans. He has faithfully carried out his part of the contract, and is warmly greeted by those whom the coming of the zouaves has saved.

Lady Ruth is pale—she has looked upon sights such as are not usually seen by her sex—sights that make strong men shudder until they become battle hardened, for war is always cruel and bloody.

"Let us get to the hotel as soon as possible," she says to Aunt Gwen.

"My goodness, are you going to faint?" exclaims that good soul.

"Oh, no, I don't think so, but the sooner I am at the hotel the better," replies the girl.

"There comes John Craig. He has been talking with the officer in command of the soldiers, and I guess has made some sort of arrangements for us."

What Aunt Gwen says is true enough, for John leads them to captured horses, and ere long they are moving in the direction of Algiers, escorted by a detachment of the zouaves on foot.

Their trials for the night are over, but they will never forget what they have seen and endured. John is secretly fuming, as he ponders over the facts. If he could only prove that Sir Lionel is the direct cause of all this trouble, he would demand satisfaction from the Briton in some shape. That is where the trouble lies, in proving it. What he has learned thus far can be put down as only suspicions or hints, though they look bad for the Briton.

If Lady Ruth has observed enough to open her eyes with regard to the veteran soldier, John will call it quits.

A thought occurs to him, even as he rides toward Algiers, that causes a grim smile to break out upon his face. It is a thought worthy of a Richelieu—an idea brilliant with possibilities.

"Here are Sir Lionel and Pauline—two despairing people who long for the unattainable. Why should they not be mated? It is perhaps possible, and would be a master stroke of genius on my part. Jove! I'll see what I can do! Great pity to have all the plotting on one side of the house."

From that hour John Craig devotes his whole mind to the accomplishment of this purpose, for he sees the benefit of diplomacy.

This is the great idea that is struggling in his mind as he rides along.

St. George Rathborne

CHAPTER XXI

SHE CALLS HIM JOHN NOW

When the news of the battle is known in Algiers, great excitement abounds. There are many sympathizers of Bab Azoun among the native population, and in some quarters their ugly teeth are shown; but France has too secure a hold of Algeria not to be ready for such an emergency, and her troops parade the streets, armed for battle.

Consequently no demonstration on the part of the natives is attempted. Among the foreigners, and in the better circles of merchants and traders, there is great rejoicing over the victory, for it has long been dangerous to travel in the region of the coast because of the bold forays of this same Bab Azoun. They hope his power will now be broken, and that perhaps the outlaw himself may be dead.

In the morning our friends gather for breakfast. John alone is absent, nor do they know what has become of him, for the clerk of the hotel informs them that the Chicagoan was early astir.

He comes in before they are done eating, but volunteers no information concerning his wanderings, so that they of course conclude he has only been for a walk.

Sir Lionel seems rather shy. Most men upon making such a dismal failure on two separate occasions, would probably be willing to give up the game, but there is something of the bull-dog about Sir Lionel. He will hold on until the end.

He fears John Craig has penetrated his schemes, and this makes him assume a dogged air. Evidently he still clings to hope of ultimate success.

As for Craig, he is undecided whether to call Sir Lionel a fool or a knave, and is rapidly drifting to a belief that the Briton may be a composite of both.

They have much to see in Algiers. Mosques, bazaars, and the remarkable features that cluster about this famous resort. A thousand and one things unite to charm a traveler who strikes Algiers in the winter time, and they usually go hence with many regrets, and memories that will never fade.

John watches his chance to speak to the girl at his side. He feels that the time has come when he must tell her what he has in his heart—that he loves her.

If she gives him his *conge*, he will go his way and try to forget; but he has hopes of a different answer; eye speaks to eye, and there is a language of the heart that needs not lips to proclaim it, a secret telegraphy that brings together those who love. The touch of a hand thrills as no other touch can, and the sound of a voice heard unexpectedly causes the heart to almost cease beating.

At length he makes an opportunity, as only a bold and determined lover can. They have gone in the street-cars to the terraced heights of Mustapha Superieur, to visit a house which most tourists see—a house with a remarkable history —and in departing, John and Lady Ruth somehow are separated from the rest. The fault lies with him, because at the last moment he proposed a final view of the wonderful scene spread out below, to which Lady Ruth consented, and as the others boarded the tram-car that would take them back to the city, John called out their intention, and that they would join them later.

There is nothing singular about this, and yet Lady Ruth's cheeks turn rosy as she hears Aunt Gwen's laugh, and stealing a glance over her shoulder discovers that quaint individual shaking her finger out of the car-window.

Upon a rustic seat the two rest. The grand panorama spread before them charms the eye, and they feast upon the glorious scene. How blue the sea appears, and the numerous sails are like splashes of white against the deep background.

There lies Algiers in all her glory, modern structures almost side by side with Mohammedan mosques, whose domes shine like great balls of gold and whose minarets guard the sacred edifice like sentries thrown out in the nature of defenses.

Who could gaze upon such a vision and not feel his heart stirred, must indeed be dead to everything that appeals to the better senses.

John Craig, M.D., might ordinarily be set down as an enthusiastic lover of nature, and such a scene when he first gazed upon it aroused the deepest emotions in his artist heart; but strange to say he pays little heed to what is before him now. It is what occupies the rustic seat in common with John Craig that takes his whole attention.

How shall he say it. What words can he frame into an animated expression of his feelings? It was all mapped out before, but the words have utterly slipped his memory, as is always the case in such events.

He turns to Lady Ruth. Her hand is in her lap. He boldly reaches out and takes it. There is only a feeble resistance. Their eyes meet, "Lady Ruth, will you give me this hand?"

"You—I—what could you do with it?" she asks, turning rosy red.

"Well, to begin with—this," and he presses it passionately to his lips.

"Oh! Doctor Craig, what if some one should see you!" now struggling to free her hand, which he holds firmly.

He laughs recklessly, this hitherto shy young man. Once in the affair, he cares little for prying eyes, and indeed there is small chance of any one noticing them in this retired spot, as there are no other sight-seers around.

"I don't care who sees me. I've got to tell you what I'm sure you already know, that I love you—I love you."

He leans forward and looks in her face, which is downcast. She has ceased to struggle now, and her hand lies fluttering in his.

Such scenes as these the novelist has no business to linger over. The emotions that are brought out at such a time should be sacred from the public gaze.

John does not wait long for his answer, as Lady Ruth is a sensible girl, and really cares a great deal more for this young man than she has been ready to admit even to herself.

So she tells him that she is afraid she does take an un-common interest in his welfare, and that perhaps it would be as well for her to later on assume such a position as will give her the right to watch over him.

So it is nicely settled, and John feels supremely happy, just as all sincere and successful wooers have done from time immemorial.

After a short time John remembers that he meant to intro-duce a certain subject, and putting aside his feelings of new-found joy—there will be plenty of time for all that—he speaks of Sir Lionel.

"Now that you know I am not at all jealous, I want to talk about another. Sir Lionel Blunt."

Her face lights up with a smile.

"Perhaps I can guess what you would say."

"It is about the affair last night."

"Poor Sir Lionel is rather quiet to-day. He is not so young as he was, and I imagine that his severe exertions last night have caused him many twinges to-day."

"Perhaps. It was the most remarkable affair I ever witnessed."

"You saw it all?"

"Yes. Mustapha and myself were in hiding not far away. We were astounded at the easy way those fellows died."

At this Lady Ruth gives a merry peal of laughter.

"It was really ridiculous."

"Did you guess it at the time?"

"Well, certain things looked very strange to me. I was amazed as we were leaving to see a man whom I was positive had twice fallen as if dead, raise his head and look after us with a smile on his ugly face.

"Whatever I thought, I was so glad to get away on any terms that I said nothing, and when the next engagement took place I found Sir Lionel very much in earnest.

"On this account, although feeling sure that he was the cause of all the trouble, I have been disposed to forgive him. You know the poor fellow professes to be in love with me, though I have had some reason to believe it is my fortune he is after as well, for my father unfortunately left me an heiress."

"Well, I'm in a position to be generous, and though I condemn his methods, I can easily see how, in his despair he might forget his honor. I have good reason to believe this is not the first time he has tried to play the hero."

Lady Ruth looks surprised.

"How is that?" she asks.

Thereupon John narrates what the boatman said to him off Malta, concerning a broken plank in the bottom of the little craft, which of course astonishes the young girl.

She shows some indignation at the thought of his imperiling her life.

"The joke of the whole thing lies in the fact that it was you who saved the would-be hero of the occasion," remarks John, and this fact induces both of them to laugh.

On the whole they feel so happy that it is hard to bear a grudge even against the veteran who has been baffled by fate.

Lady Ruth cannot forget that Sir Lionel gave many evidences of being in love with her, and a woman is apt to forgive even a fault in a man who professes to have sinned for her, to have even given up honor in the hope of winning her favor.

"I have arranged a little scheme whereby I hope to pay Sir Lionel back in his own coin," says the young Chicagoan, grimly.

"Why, John, I thought you said just now that you could forgive him. Now you pretend to be quite blood-thirsty."

"Oh, no; not that. I'm looking out for the poor fellow. He's gone it alone quite long enough, and I want to see him caught."

"Caught? Explain, please. Perhaps I'm a little obtuse, but really, under the circumstances—"

"Yes, I know. It's all excusable, my dear girl. In plain English I want to see the veteran married."

"Married?"

"And I shall take upon myself the task of selecting the girl who will rule him hereafter."

"John, what do you mean? Surely—oh, that is nonsense. Tell

me who she is?"

"Pauline Potter," calmly.

"Why, that's the actress."

"True."

"The actress who professed to be so madly in love with one Doctor John Craig."

"And as the said Craig is already taken, she is left out in the cold. Now you behold my little scheme. We are happy—why should not these two people be the same?"

"Why, indeed?"

"Their greatest fault lies in loving not wisely but too well. This has caused them to sin. Now, in order to prevent any future plots that may give us trouble, I purpose to so arrange it that Sir Lionel shall have a wife and Pauline a husband."

"A clever idea."

"I may want your assistance."

"You can have it at any time."

"We must protect ourselves, and the easiest way to do this will be to disarm our foes."

"Really, Doctor Chicago, I didn't give you credit for so much shrewdness. Tell me if you have any plans arranged."

"Well, only the skeleton of one as yet, but I'll tell you all about it as far as I have gone."

They sit upon that bench for a full hour. Time is not taken into account when love rules the occasion.

It is Lady Ruth who finally jumps up with a cry of consternation. She has heard a clock upon a tower in new Algiers strike the hour.

"What will they think of us, John?" she says.

"Little I care, for I mean to announce our engagement to Aunt Gwen on sight, and she is the only one who has any business to complain," returns the successful wooer, firmly.

"Oh! it is so sudden; perhaps we'd better wait a little while."

"With your permission, not an hour. You belong to me, now—see, let me put this solitaire diamond on your finger. It was my mother's ring. By that token I simply desire to warn all men 'hands off.' Tell me, am I right, Ruth?"

"Yes; I can offer no objection. Do as you think best, doctor."

This is a beautiful beginning. Clouds will be rare in their future if they keep on in this way.

So they once more go back to the hotel, and find Aunt Gwen on the lookout, her kindly face wearing an anxious expression that becomes a quizzical one when she sees John smile.

"Your blessing, Aunt Gwen," he says.

"My what?"

"Oh! it's all settled. Ruth has promised to be my wife," continues John, looking very happy.

"The dickens she has!" and Philander pushes into view from behind the voluminous skirts of his better half. "What business has she to accept any one without consulting her doting—"

"Philander!"

"—Aunt? Don't take me seriously, my boy. Accept my congratulations, wish you joy, and thank Heaven it isn't that pompous baronet."

"Amen!" says John, warmly.

"Now that you allow me a chance, Philander, I want to say just this: it suits me to a dot. I'm delighted—enchanted. Of course you'll live in Chicago. That's another blow against John Bull. We'll be mistress of the seas yet. Here, let me kiss you both, my children, and take the blessing of a woman who has not lived fifty years for nothing."

CHAPTER XXII

THE WEAVER—FATE!

Even in the midst of his happiness John Craig has not forgotten the one important fact that brought him to Algiers.

While he can devote himself to laying a plan for the accomplishment of a certain object, and with the assistance of Lady Ruth arrange to surprise Sir Lionel Blunt, he is at the same time anxiously awaiting news.

Will old Ben Taleb carry out his promise? The heart of the young man beats high with hope.

Unconscious of a great surprise in store for him, John enters the hotel with Lady Ruth.

"A gentleman in the parlor to see you, sir."

John's face flashes; the instantaneous thought flashes into his mind that a messenger has at length come from the Moorish doctor.

He enters.

His eyes are dazzled a little by the glare of the sun on white buildings, and the room is dim. A man's figure advances toward him. Surely that step is familiar. Good heavens, what a shock comes upon him!

"Father!"

"John, my boy!"

He has believed this father to be at the other side of the world. He is surprised at the warmth of the greeting he receives. Really, this is quite unlike the proud man John has known all his life, a man who seemed to ever surround himself with a wall of coldness.

A sudden shock runs through John's frame. It is as if he has been given the negative and positive ends of a battery. He believes that his mother is here, in this city. Can that have anything to do with his father's coming?

A feeling of resentment springs up, then dies away as he gets a good look at his parent's face.

"Father, what has happened? Have you failed; has any disaster come upon us?"

"Why do you ask that, John?"

"Your face; it is changed so. I miss something I have been accustomed to see there."

Duncan Craig smiles.

"Ah! John, my boy, please Heaven, I am changed. I have been humbled in the dust, and I believe I have emerged from the furnace, I trust, a far better man."

John is puzzled. He cannot make out what has caused this humbling on the part of his proud paternal ancestor, nor is he able to hazard a guess as to the effect it may have upon his fortunes.

Craig, Sr., does not explain what brings him to Algiers at this particular time, but immediately starts asking questions regarding the scenes John has gazed upon since leaving the German college of medicine where he received his graduation diploma.

While they are yet talking, who should appear on the scene but Lady Ruth.

"You carried off my fan, John, and I wanted to mend it while I had the chance. Oh! I beg your pardon; I did not know you were engaged. The clerk told me you were in here, but—"

John has eagerly darted forward and has hold of the fair girl's arm.

"I want to introduce some one to you, some one you would see sooner or later. Sir, this is Lady Ruth Stanhope, a young lady to whom I have lost my heart, and my promised wife."

"What!" exclaimed Craig, Sr., "bless my soul, you're only a boy, John."

"Twenty-three, sir," promptly.

"Yes, you're right. Time flies. You've given me quite a little shock, but, by Jove! I'm already favorably impressed with your taste. Will you allow me the privilege of a kiss, my dear?"

"Sir!" indignantly, for in the dim light she does not see that his mustache is snow-white, as is also his hair.

Her tragic attitude rather alarms John.

"Ruth, it's my father!" he cries.

This alters the case.

"Your father! Oh! John, has he—" She sees the warning finger her betrothed raises up, and stops suddenly, for she has been about to say something relative to the presence of Sister Magdalen in the city.

The elder Craig raises the shade, and in the new light Lady Ruth sees a remarkably handsome man of middle age, even distinguished in his manner.

Then he is John's father, too, and that makes quite a difference. She approaches, with hand extended.

"Forgive me, sir. I did not dream John's father was within five thousand miles of Algiers."

"And if you have agreed to be my only boy's wife you must be my daughter, too."

This time he bestows a paternal salute upon her velvety cheek. Possibly Lady Ruth is ready to believe she is entering the Craig family very rapidly; but with a woman's idea of the eternal fitness of small things, she feels very much pleased to know that her future father-in-law is such a distinguished-looking gentleman.

As is proper, she excuses herself, and leaves the room. Doubtless father and son have much to talk over.

When John finds himself alone with the parent for whom he has ever felt the greatest respect without deep filial affection, he grows anxious again.

What can have brought the other across the sea at this particular time? Is it connected with the facts he cherishes; the presence of this other one in Algiers? and if so, what does Duncan Craig mean to do; cut him off with a penny because he has dared allow the longing in his heart to have its way, and has endeavored to find the mother so long lost?

When he steals another look at the elder Craig's face, he cannot see that there is anything like deep anger there, and yet John admits that he is not a good hand at analyzing motives.

He dares not mention the matter himself, and is therefore bound to wait until his respected father speaks, if he does so at all.

Craig, Sr., talks of his trip, declares he is delighted with the glimpse he has had of Algiers, and wonders how it would pay a good doctor to settle down there for the winter months; at which John declares it would just suit him.

Then the other drops a gentle clew to his late movements by asking John which arm it was upon which he was recently vaccinated, which is a puzzler to the young fellow until the name of Malta is mentioned, when he cries:

"Were you at Valetta, father?"

"I reached there two days after you left. Bless me, the whole town was still talking over a brave deed that had recently saved a child's life."

"Nonsense!"

"Well, it pleased me when I heard the name of the young man who saved the child at the risk of his own life. I was proud to know I was his father."

Still no mention of the real cause that has brought him so far from home. John is baffled.

His recent happiness is dimmed a little, and he has an uneasy feeling as though the unknown were about to happen; a weight rests upon his heart.

A strange thing occurs. Sir Lionel passes the door, and immediately Craig, Sr., is taken with a spasm of fury. He acts as if to start to rush out, then faces his son. John sees his father's face for the first time convulsed with fury.

"Do you know that man?" he demands.

"Certainly."

"Is his name Blunt?"

"Yes, sir."

"I thought I could not be mistaken. There is something singular that brings him here at this time. John, is this Reginald Blunt a particular friend of yours?"

"Why, no, sir, in fact, he was my rival for the hand of Ruth Stanhope. But you call him Reginald; this is Sir Lionel Blunt, a colonel from India and the south of Africa."

"Then I made a mistake. It is his cousin. Yet I knew the face; I knew the face."

Again John wonders.

"Did a Blunt ever do you a wrong, father?"

"Yes, I have believed so these many years; have been ready to stake my very life upon it; and yet, and yet. Heaven forgive me for what wicked thoughts I have hugged to my heart."

These words arouse a wild hope in the mind of John Craig. Can it be possible his father has after all these years seen light?

The idea is so wonderful that, although hope causes his heart to beat like a trip-hammer, he remains silent. When the time comes, Craig, Sr., will speak; he knows this of old.

Later on, when John finds himself alone, he begins to think again of the little scheme he has decided to work, for the edification of himself and the future good of Sir Lionel Blunt—ditto Mademoiselle Pauline, the tragedy queen.

It must be well carried out to produce the intended effect, for these are more than ordinarily sensible people and might resent the interference of outsiders in their private affairs.

Whatever happens must not appear to have been prearranged, but be purely accidental.

Perhaps success may come; it is worth an effort at any rate.

John fears more than ever lest Pauline, in the bitterness of her anger, attempt some injury toward the girl he loves and who has made the sweet confession that he is very dear to her.

This causes him much more uneasiness than anything else ever did. He can feel afraid for the safety of Ruth where he would not dream of allowing the sensation on his own account.

Hence his anxiety to mature his plans and clear the path ahead.

In the perfected work he believes he can count on the assistance of Mustapha Cadi. The Arab guide has already proved himself so valuable a man that John is ready to trust him with nearly anything.

So he waits to hear of some message from the old Moorish doctor, and while waiting begins to arrange in his mind the plans for a future campaign.

Pauline is still at the hotel, for he has had a glimpse of her. The actress does not seem very much discouraged by the disasters of the past. She smiles on meeting John, and nods in a cheery way, as though giving him to understand that she is not done with him yet. He feels that he can afford to meet her in the same spirit, although anxious about his Ruth.

Fortune favors him, too.

The British nobleman happens to be standing near as Pauline sweeps past, and as is her professional habit she gives him a bright look, that somehow starts the blood to bounding in the veteran's veins.

He approaches John.

"Pardon me, but did you bow to that lady, my dear doctor?"

John admits that he did, though careful not to show any

unusual eagerness about it.

"May I ask who she is?"

"Come! this is rather singular."

"What is?"

"Why, truth to tell, I believe the lady is already interested in you."

"In me?"

Sir Lionel at once puffs out a little, as though feeling conesquential. It is gratifying to his conceit to hear that this beautiful being has actually taken notice of him.

"Well, it would not be right for me to say more," continues the diplomatic young man, and this increases the curiosity of the soldier.

"Who is she, doctor?"

"One of the most noted beauties on the American stage," replies John.

"An actress?"

"Yes, and a clever one; very popular in the States, and highly respected. Why, she set half the young men in Chicago wild a year or two ago."

"Including yourself, doctor?" slyly.

"I acknowledge the corn, Sir Lionel. Young men have no show to win her favor."

"Indeed."

"She prefers a gentleman of middle age. A man who has seen life and had varied experiences."

"Wise girl."

"In short, Sir Lionel, Pauline Potter is an admirer of bravery; she adores a soldier who has won his spurs."

"Ahem! Pauline is a favorite name of mine. I've read of her triumphs, too. She was out in Melbourne two years or more ago and carried the town by storm."

"That is a fact."

"Duse take it, d'ye know what I've half a mind to do?"

"What's that, Sir Lionel?" asks John, with a very sober face, but secretly chuckling at the success that is meeting him half-way. Why, he has hardly dug his pit before the baronet comes tumbling into it.

"I've a good notion to strike up a flirtation with Mademoiselle Pauline, to relieve the tedium of the hours. Who knows what result it might have?" thinking that perhaps such a move might arouse a feeling of jealousy in Lady Ruth's heart, and thus disclose to herself the state of her feelings.

"Who knows, indeed? Be careful, Sir Lionel. Pauline is a bewitching creature. She may add your heart to her list of conquests."

"Well, if I entered the lists, I'd give as good as I received," complacently stroking his luxuriant mustache.

"Jove! I really believe you would. And I'm human enough, having adored the bright star in vain, to wish that some one else might cause the beautiful Pauline to feel some of the pangs she gave us. If the notion strikes you, colonel, I wish you success."

Then John immediately branches out upon another subject.

The seed is sown. It will require a little time to germinate, and then perhaps the result may prove satisfactory.

So much for a beginning.

When John finds himself alone, he sets to work trying to kindle a counter irritant, a congenial flame that will burn in the heart of the actress.

Securing a beautiful bouquet of flowers he fastens to them a card upon which he has written in a hand somewhat like the bold chirography of the veteran, the words:

"A compliment to beauty and histrionic renown."

This he first shows to Lady Ruth.

Then a servant is hired to take it to the room of Pauline Potter, and he is to utterly refuse any information beyond the fact that a gentleman paid him to do it.

Of course this will excite the curiosity of the actress, and further developments may soon be expected.

John, in a secure corner, waits, nor does he have long to watch before Pauline appears, going straight to the desk where lies the ponderous tome in which have registered men of note from all over the world.

She is looking for a signature that will in some degree at least correspond with the writing of the note found among the flowers. Only a few minutes she remains there, and then turning away, gives the watchful John a chance to see the smile on her face.

Pauline has, as she believes, discovered the identity of the unknown who sent the flowers.

The little side plot works apace, since each of them already feels an interest in the other. The flame being kindled, the fire will grow of its own accord.

He believes he can turn his attention to other things if necessary.

The remainder of the day is put in with sight-seeing. John notes one thing. Sir Lionel leaves them after a time and saunters back to the hotel. When this occurs, Lady Ruth and the doctor exchange significant looks. They understand that already the seed is beginning to sprout, and the absence of the Englishman is a positive relief to them.

Duncan Craig accompanies the party. Aunt Gwen has already taken a great fancy to the gentleman, and makes it as pleasant for him as possible.

John tries to study his father in secret, but finds it a hard task.

Craig, Sr., is a lawyer of repute in Chicago, a man with a large income. He has been called a Sphinx, and well deserves the cognomen, for no man shows less upon his face the emotions of his heart.

Only in debate, and when addressing a jury that hangs breathlessly upon his words, does he drop the mask and show what fire is in his soul.

So John, as in times of old, is unable to fathom the depths of his father's thoughts.

He is wretched, not knowing whether the coming of Craig, Sr., will influence his mission for good or evil.

And still the expected message from Ben Taleb does not come.

Once more evening vails day's splendor, and another night approaches, a night that John hopes will make a change in this monotonous run of luck, and bring him news.

Imagine his astonishment and secret delight when an open carriage stops at the door of the hotel, and as he glances at the elegant couple seated therein discovers Sir Lionel and the Potter.

It almost takes his breath away.

"Well, he is a hurricane in love, I declare. If he fought in the same way, the Victoria cross wouldn't be enough to decorate him. Jove! they already are dead set, each with the other. That was the cleverest piece of business I ever attempted. If success comes, I'll have to set up as a match-maker."

How gallantly Sir Lionel assists the lovely actress from the vehicle, as if he expects that the whole town may be watching.

Doubtless his actions are in part studied with a view to the effect upon a certain person, nameless, who must assuredly be looking from her chamber window above.

In that case he is apt to go too far, and soon find himself in the wiles of Pauline, who, accustomed to playing with men as one might the pieces on a chess-board, would have little trouble in manipulating one Englishman, fresh from the wilds of South Africa.

So John rests on his oars and waits for the chance to come; and the unseen hand that weaves the fabric of their lives, manipulates the shuttle through the woof.

CHAPTER XXIII

FOUND—IN THE HOUSE OF THE MOOR

John hears at last.

A native servant brings him a note, and it can be set down as positive that the young Chicagoan eagerly breaks the seal.

It is from Ben Taleb. He writes a fair English hand, for he is a man of much education.

"Come again this night at eleven. Tell Mustapha to be at the wall where you departed from my house, at that hour, and to rap upon the large stone with the handle of his knife, giving the signal of Mahomet's tomb.

"Ben Taleb, of Morocco."

So John's heart thrills with expectation. This looks friendly; he may be near the end of his journey. It is still dark and uncertain ahead, for even when he has found his mother, a reconciliation between these separated parents seems impossible. The past has too much of bitterness in it to be easily put aside.

His first thought is of Mustapha, and he casts around for the

Arab, whom he last saw close by the door of the hotel.

The dusky courier is near by, engaged in a little game with several companion guides, for the Arab as a rule loves gaming, and will risk everything but his horse.

When Mustapha catches his eye he comes up hastily, understanding there is something in the wind.

"We are to go again into the old town."

"When, monsieur?"

"This night. See! Ben Taleb has sent me a message."

The Arab looks at the paper stolidly; it might as well be Sanscrit to him.

"Read it, monsieur."

So John complies, and his guide takes in all that is said. He nods his head to show that he understands.

"This time I, too, will change my appearance, and they will not know that it is Mustapha Cadi who walks through the lanes of old Al Jezira with an unbeliever at his side."

"A bright thought, Mustapha. When shall we leave the hotel?"

"Say half past nine, meet me here. I will have all arranged. The *burnoose* is safe."

John prepares for business.

He remembers that on the previous occasion he had need of

weapons—that they came very near an encounter with the natives—and hence arms himself.

Before quitting the hotel he feels it incumbent upon himself to see Lady Ruth, and tell her where he is going. Nothing like beginning early, you know. She has already commenced to control his destiny.

Lady Ruth has a headache, and is bathing her brow with cologne in the privacy of her little boudoir parlor, but readily consents to see the young man.

"You'll think me a fright, John, with my hair brushed back like this"—John stops this in a thrice as any ardent lover might, taking advantage of the professor's absence, and the fact that Aunt Gwen has gone back in the second room for another chair—"but once in a great while I have a headache that will only succumb to a certain process. You will excuse me?"

"Indeed, I sympathize with you; have had the same splitting headache myself more than a few times. I wouldn't have intruded—"

"You know it's no intrusion, John," with reproach in her eyes.

"Kind of you to say so, my dear, but to the point I have heard from Ben Taleb."

"Oh! your face tells me it is good news."

"I am to visit him at ten."

"To-night?"

"Yes."

"But John, the danger. You yourself told me it was no little thing to enter old Al Jezira in the night. Those narrow lanes, with strange figures here and there, eying one fiercely; the houses that threaten to topple over on one's head; all these things make it a risky place to wander in even during the daytime. After dark it must be awful."

So John describes the plan of action, and interests his affianced, who asks more questions about his former visit, not forgetting the marvelous beauty of the Moor's daughter, for she is human.

Time flies under such circumstances, and hence it is John suddenly exclaims:

"I declare, it's after nine o'clock."

"And my headache is gone."

At this both laugh.

"You must be a wizard, John, to charm it away so completely," she declares.

"I trust I shall always be as successful in the days to come," breathes John, and this of course causes a blush to sweep over the fair maid's face.

He hurries to his room to prepare for what is before him. Deep in his heart arises a prayer for success. Again that feeling of anticipation sweeps over him. Remembering former disappointments, he endeavors to subdue his hopes and to prepare for another set back, but this does not prevent him at times from indulging in dreams of happiness.

It is just half-past nine when he reaches the door of the hotel.

Mustapha Cadi is there, looking confident and bearing a small bundle. Again, in a dark corner, John assumes an Arab covering, while his conductor proceeds to alter his own looks so that any whom they meet may not know who the tall Arab is.

So they tread the lanes of the hill-side town. Just as on the previous night, they meet Arabs, Moors, Kabyles, Jews and negroes. The silence is like that of the tomb, and yet the interior of more than one house doubtless presents a spectacle gay enough to please any lover of light and color, of lovely women, of rippling fountains, sweet flowers that load the air with their incense, and all the accessories a Moorish court can devise, for these people, while keeping the exterior of their dwellings plain, spend money lavishly upon the interior.

Now they are at the wall, and Mustapha gives the signal clearly; indeed, John fancies the hilt of the knife meets the stone with more force than is necessary, or else his ears deceive him.

The signal is heard, is answered, and in another minute they are inside the wall.

As they walk along behind their guide John whispers to the Arab:

"On my word, I believe the fellow neglected to quite secure the door in the wall," to which remark Mustapha replies in low tones:

"Presumably he knows his business, monsieur; anyhow, it concerns us not at all."

Which John takes as a gentle reminder that these Arabs are very particular not to interfere with things that belong to another.

He says no more.

They reach the central room, opening upon the court where plashes the fountain.

The guide stops.

Upon the scented air comes the notes of a musical instrument, a mandolin, and the chords are peculiarly sad and yet so very full of music.

Then a voice breaks forth—such singing John has heard only in his dreams—it is a voice of wondrous power, sympathetic and sweet, a voice that would haunt a man forever.

John knows no Moorish maidens can sing that song, and his heart gives a wild throb as the conviction is suddenly forced upon him that at last, after these weary years of waiting, after his search over half the world, he is now listening to the voice that hushed his infantile cries, and fell upon his ears like a benison.

No wonder, then, he stands there as if made of stone—stands and drinks in the sweet volume of sound as it floods that Moorish court, until the last note dies away as might the carol of a bird at even-tide.

Then he swallows a sob, and braces himself for the coming ordeal. Something behind reaches his ear. He is positive he catches a deep groan as of despair; perhaps it comes from some cage, where this Moorish judge has an enemy in confinement.

He is not given a chance to speculate upon the subject. His guide touches his arm and points. John discovers that his presence has already been made known to the Moor.

He is expected to come forward. Under the circumstances, the young man is in no condition for delay. That song, that heavenly voice, has gone straight to his heart, and he longs to look upon the face of the sweet singer.

So he advances, not slowly and with any show of dignity, but in the eager way that does credit to his heart.

He sees a figure in black, seated near the old Moor, and instantly his eyes are glued upon that face.

Then his heart tells him he now looks upon the face of the mother who has been lost to him so long.

Does she know? has she received his note, or is her presence here simply at the desire of her friend, the old Moor? She does not show any intense excitement as he approaches, and this tends to make him believe she has been kept in ignorance of the truth.

The Mohammedan doctor and his lovely daughter watch his advance with deep interest, for they are human, and take pleasure in a good deed done. The Koran commends it just as thoroughly as does our Bible. At the same time slaves are in waiting near by, armed with deadly cimeters, and should it prove that John has deceived them, that the Sister does not greet him with love, but fear, because he bears the name of Craig, a signal from Ben Taleb will be the signing of his death warrant.

John fastens his eyes hungrily upon the face he now sees. He stands distant only a yard or so, and as yet has not uttered a syllable, only waiting to see if his burning gaze, his looks of eager love and devotion, will have a miraculous effect on his parent.

As he stands thus mutely before her, she becomes aware of his presence for the first time. She looks up at his face, the casual glance becomes immediately a stare; her cheeks grow pale as death; it is evident that something has aroused memories of the past, and they flood her soul.

Slowly the woman arises. Her figure is slight, but there is a nobility about it. Purity is written upon her brow, in her eyes shines the light of faith that dares to look the whole world in the face. And before a word is spoken John Craig knows his mother has been dreadfully wronged in the past, suffering in silence because of some noble motive.

She has gained her feet, and now advances, walking like one in a dream, her hands outstretched. No wonder; it is like a phantasy, this seeing a loved face of the past in the home of a Moor in Algiers. She must indeed think it an illusion.

Now her hand touches John's face. Imagine the intense thrill that sweeps over his frame at the impact. Soul speaks to soul, heart answers heart.

The woman begins to tremble. The look of frightened wonder upon her face gives way to one of astonishment.

"It is no illusion! Alive! Oh, what does this mean? Where am I? Who are you?"

Thus the broken sentences fell from her lips, as though she hardly knows what she says.

John can only think of one reply, and as he puts out his

hands, his whole heart is contained in the whispered words:

"Oh, my mother!"

This seems to break the spell. In another instant she has eagerly clasped her arms around his neck.

"Heaven be praised; my prayer is answered. My child has sought me out."

It is the magic power of love.

John's face tells his great joy. Words are denied them for some little time, but with brimming eyes they gaze into each other's face.

"Oh! mother, I have searched for you in many lands. For years I have longed to see you, to tell you that my heart believed in you. By the kindness of Heaven, that time has come."

"And you, my own boy, you believe me innocent, worthy of your love, though the world called me guilty?" she murmurs.

"Yes, because of the great love I bear you, I would believe it against all. Oh! my mother, how barren my life has been, without your companionship, your love. Many, many nights I have wept bitter tears of anguish to think of you somewhere upon the face of the earth, wandering alone, because of circumstantial evidence."

Again from the darkness beyond the court, comes that deep, terrible groan. The old Moor turns his head as though he does not understand it; but the tableau in front is too dramatic to be lost.

"I began to believe I should have to quit this world of woes without seeing you, for though I do not wish to disturb your happiness, my poor boy, you must see from my looks that I am fading like a flower in the fall; that the monster, consumption, is sapping my life. Still, I may live some years to enjoy your love; be of good cheer. How strange to see you a man grown, you whom I left almost a babe. And, John, you so closely resemble, as I knew him then, your father, my poor deceived Duncan, whom Heaven knows I have never ceased to remember with love; who wronged me terribly, but the circumstances were fearfully against me. Heaven has purified my heart by suffering."

"I can stand this no longer!" cries a voice, and a man rushes into view, advancing until he stands before them. "My eyes have been opened to the truth. In bitter tears I repent the sorrowful past. Blanche, behold your husband, unworthy to kiss the hem of your garment."

CHAPTER XXIV

CONCLUSION

John has been so amazed at the sight of this newcomer that he can not move a hand or foot. He immediately recognizes his father, of course, but the fact of Duncan Craig being present in this place is what temporarily paralyzes him.

The coming of the other creates a decided sensation; it can be easily understood. Upon the unfortunate wife and mother the effect is most marked.

Many years have passed since last she saw this man, her husband. Circumstances caused her to incur his apparently righteous anger, to be sent out into the world as one unworthy to bear his name.

All this she has borne meekly, doing good wherever Heaven chose to send her. The terrible infliction has tried her soul, and she has been purified as by fire.

After this life suffering she now finds this husband at her feet. His proud spirit is broken, and he seeks forgiveness.

She has long since learned to put away the ordinary small feelings that actuate so many of her sex; but being still human, she cannot but feel gratified at the vindication that has come.

John holds his breath and awaits the outcome of this strange event. He remembers the sudden rage of the old Moor on the previous occasion, when he told him he was a Craig, and fully expects to hear something from the same source again.

Nor is he mistaken.

Ben Taleb has been listening intently, and not a word of what has passed escapes his ear. He catches the confession of the man who humbles himself, and his eyes blaze.

Almost immediately he claps his hands, and half a dozen armed retainers make their appearance, springing from some unknown quarter.

"You have dared enter my house. You, a Craig, who brought years of suffering upon the woman we revere. It is well. Allah has sent you here. Mohammed is satisfied to leave you to our hands. I will be merciful, as the hyena is merciful. Instead of having you torn to pieces I will order you shot. You will learn that a Moor knows how to avenge the wrongs of one for whom he entertains feelings of gratitude."

His words are cutting and cruel, and John, expecting every second to see the slaves make their savage assault upon his father, holds himself in readiness to jump forward and assist him.

The situation is indeed critical.

It looks as though a very trifling matter would precipitate a riot, in which deadly weapons must be used.

St. George Rathborne

Duncan Craig has made a terrible mistake in his past. He has been known as a cold, proud man, though much of this has been assumed in order to deceive himself. Yet no one ever called him a coward.

He knows that bodily danger menaces him, and as a soldier his spirit is at once in arms.

Springing to his feet, he faces the old Moor.

His arms are folded. Upon his face can be seen a defiant light.

"I have entered your house, Ben Taleb, unarmed, bent upon a mission of love. To humble myself. You may have the power to crush me. I have done what I believed to be right just as soon as the light of truth entered my soul. The consequences may be disastrous, but I am ready to meet them."

The old Moor is struck by his manner, but, still moved by the passion that swept over him at mention of that name, he does not allow his anger to abate a particle.

"Because of the past you shall suffer. You have ruined the life of this woman, whose only fault was in loving you, a base, heartless dog. Say your prayers, wretched man, for you have but a few minutes to live."

He faces his judge calmly. An American can meet death with even the stoicism so characteristic of the Moslem race.

The terrible sentence has awakened one who has seemed to be in a stupor. Sister Magdalen arouses herself. The old feelings within her heart are not dead; they have only been slumbering all this while.

She steps between Duncan Craig and the Moor, her face shining with a new light. She raises her hand as if to ward off the impending blow, and her voice is sweet and gentle.

"Ali Ben Taleb, great is thy house and the blessings of Allah hang over it. I understand the motive that prompts you to thus undertake to avenge what you think are my wrongs. But you must halt. I demand a hearing."

"Speak on; my ears are open to your voice. You saved my child from the pestilence that stalketh at noon day, and the heart of Ben Taleb has been full of gratitude ever since," replies the dignified native doctor.

"First, then, hear that, though I thought I should die when I no longer had a home in my husband's house, my eyes were speedily opened, and I saw that Heaven was using me as an instrument to bring about good. So I learned to be patient. Confident of my innocence, I could calmly await the time when the truth would be made known. That hour, Ali Ben Taleb, has come.

"The second point, which I particularly desire to impress upon your mind, is this: You are pleased to say that I was instrumental in snatching your beloved child from the jaws of death. Be it so. Consider, then, what would have been the result had this misfortune never happened to me, if I had always remained in my husband's home."

"Great is Allah, and Mohammed is his prophet, but I fear I should have lost my child," declares the Moor.

"You see the ways of Allah are past finding out. I have long since learned to trust myself to the guidance of a power stronger than human arms.

"You talk of avenging my wrongs, but time has already done that. The result you see here in the actions of my husband. If I forgive him freely and fully, what right have you or any other person to hate him and declare vengeance? Does your Koran teach that; did Mohammed propagate such doctrines?"

The old Moor hangs his head.

"It is not for Ben Taleb to go against the will of the one who saved his child. Take, then, his miserable life, oh, remarkable woman; and as for me, I have learned a lesson."

Again he claps his hands, and the armed retainers disappear. Peace once more smiles upon the scene.

Sister Magdalen turns to her husband, and they converse in low tones, yet with an earnestness that leaves no room for doubt of their sincerity.

Presently John sees his father motion, and he joins them.

"My boy, your mother has forgiven me. Heaven knows I do not merit such action, but she is an earthly angel. And I want to ask you if you can also forgive me, because through my actions you have all these years been deprived of a mother's love?"

His contrite manner, his dejected attitude—these things would go far toward influencing John even were his heart hardened toward the unfortunate author of all this misery, which it is not.

"Ah! father, with such an example before me how could I entertain hard feelings? The past is gone. Why should we live in it. Better that we look forward toward the future and endeavor to find happiness. You know Heaven works in a mysterious way, and much good has come to the world at large through our suffering."

"Then you do forgive, my boy?"

"There is nothing to forgive, sir. Let us strive to forget the past and hope that years of happiness may be before us."

"Ah! John, you have her spirit," sighs his father, as he wrings his boy's hand.

Sister Magdalen smiles sweetly and sadly, for she knows full well that their time together in this world will be short. She does not wish to cast a damper on their present joy, however, and hence says nothing.

The Moor has been greatly impressed by all this. He learns a lesson in life, for, as a rule, the female element in oriental circles has very little to do with the events that occur from day to day, and never engage in any of the discussions upon the leading questions of the hour.

Later on the little party leave the house of Ali Ben Taleb. Their passage through the streets is accomplished in safety, for the Moor sees to it that all are well disguised.

John never learns the truth about the coming of his father. He has reason to believe that Mustapha Cadi must have entered into some arrangement of the older Craig, after hearing his story, although the stolid face of the Arab never betrays his secret.

When Lady Ruth learns that the end has come, and John's quest is at an end, she rejoices with him.

Another day in Algiers.

St. George Rathborne

Then a steamer will be due, upon which they can take passage for France, and later on reach America.

Duncan Craig is very subdued, and intensely devoted to his recovered wife. They have long conversations alone, and all that has passed in the years of their separation is told. Craig opens his heart and reveals his inmost feelings. He tells how he suffered in spirit while showing a proud face to the world, and finally how he came to learn the truth.

John becomes interested in the courtship of Sir Lionel, who, finding his ardent affection returned, pursues his game with such intensity of purpose that he wins.

Seeing them come out of a church that afternoon, Doctor Chicago is influenced to enter, and to his particular gratification learns that a ceremony has just been performed that effectually removes both of them from his track.

When he tells this to Lady Ruth that lively young lady is greatly pleased, and laughs again and again. Thus all obstacles crumble before the path of true love. Their skies are sunny and bright with hope.

Duncan Craig's wife has not become united with an order in bonds that are indissoluble. She changes her garb, but her heart has become so wedded to the work that the probabilities are she will finish her life in the sweet service of charity; and Craig, filled with penitence and newly awakened love, will be only too glad to follow her everywhere, seconding by his money, her efforts.

John means to fling his shingle to the breeze, and start upon the road of life as a full-fledged doctor. His German education will push him forward, for their system is more thorough than the American, and few there are who come out at twenty-three.

He will be separated from Miss Caprice a few months, but she is coming over to see the World's Fair, and remain. Thus Chicago gains though England loses.

With their departure from Algiers on the steamer, we may as well bid them adieu. On board they meet Sir Lionel and his wife, of whom he is at present very proud, but they keep by themselves, for each has a secret that is not for the other to know.

THE END

Choose from Thousands of 1stWorldLibrary Classics By

A. M. Barnard	Booth Tarkington	Edward Everett Hale
Ada Leverson	Boyd Cable	Edward J. O'Biren
Adolphus William Ward	Bram Stoker	Edward S. Ellis
Aesop	C. Collodi	Edwin L. Arnold
Agatha Christie	C. E. Orr	Eleanor Atkins
Alexander Aaronsohn	C. M. Ingleby	Eleanor Hallowell Abbott
Alexander Kielland	Carolyn Wells	Eliot Gregory
Alexandre Dumas	Catherine Parr Traill	Elizabeth Gaskell
Alfred Gatty	Charles A. Eastman	Elizabeth McCracken
Alfred Ollivant	Charles Amory Beach	Elizabeth Von Arnim
Alice Duer Miller	Charles Dickens	Ellem Key
Alice Turner Curtis	Charles Dudley Warner	Emerson Hough
Alice Dunbar	Charles Farrar Browne	Emilie F. Carlen
Allen Chapman	Charles Ives	Emily Bronte
Alleyne Ireland	Charles Kingsley	Emily Dickinson
Ambrose Bierce	Charles Klein	Enid Bagnold
Amelia E. Barr	Charles Hanson Towne	Enilor Macartney Lane
Amory H. Bradford	Charles Lathrop Pack	Erasmus W. Jones
Andrew Lang	Charles Romyn Dake	Ernie Howard Pie
Andrew McFarland Davis	Charles Whibley	Ethel May Dell
Andy Adams	Charles Willing Beale	Ethel Turner
Angela Brazil	Charlotte M. Braeme	Ethel Watts Mumford
Anna Alice Chapin	Charlotte M. Yonge	Eugene Sue
Anna Sewell	Charlotte Perkins Stetson	Eugenie Foa
Annie Besant	Clair W. Hayes	Eugene Wood
Annie Hamilton Donnell	Clarence Day Jr.	Eustace Hale Ball
Annie Payson Call	Clarence E. Mulford	Evelyn Everett-green
Annie Roe Carr	Clemence Housman	Everard Cotes
Annonaymous	Confucius	F. H. Cheley
Anton Chekhov	Coningsby Dawson	F. J. Cross
Archibald Lee Fletcher	Cornelis DeWitt Wilcox	F. Marion Crawford
Arnold Bennett	Cyril Burleigh	Fannie E. Newberry
Arthur C. Benson	D. H. Lawrence	Federick Austin Ogg
Arthur Conan Doyle	Daniel Defoe	Ferdinand Ossendowski
Arthur M. Winfield	David Garnett	Fergus Hume
Arthur Ransome	Dinah Craik	Florence A. Kilpatrick
Arthur Schnitzler	Don Carlos Janes	Fremont B. Deering
Arthur Train	Donald Keyhoe	Francis Bacon
Atticus	Dorothy Kilner	Francis Darwin
B.H. Baden-Powell	Dougan Clark	Frances Hodgson Burnett
B. M. Bower	Douglas Fairbanks	Frances Parkinson Keyes
B. C. Chatterjee	E. Nesbit	Frank Gee Patchin
Baroness Emmuska Orczy	E. P. Roe	Frank Harris
Baroness Orczy	E. Phillips Oppenheim	Frank Jewett Mather
Basil King	E. S. Brooks	Frank L. Packard
Bayard Taylor	Earl Barnes	Frank V. Webster
Ben Macomber	Edgar Rice Burroughs	Frederic Stewart Isham
Bertha Muzzy Bower	Edith Van Dyne	Frederick Trevor Hill
Bjornstjerne Bjornson	Edith Wharton	Frederick Winslow Taylor

Friedrich Kerst
Friedrich Nietzsche
Fyodor Dostoyevsky
G.A. Henty
G.K. Chesterton
Gabrielle E. Jackson
Garrett P. Serviss
Gaston Leroux
George A. Warren
George Ade
Geroge Bernard Shaw
George Cary Eggleston
George Durston
George Ebers
George Eliot
George Gissing
George MacDonald
George Meredith
George Orwell
George Sylvester Viereck
George Tucker
George W. Cable
George Wharton James
Gertrude Atherton
Gordon Casserly
Grace E. King
Grace Gallatin
Grace Greenwood
Grant Allen
Guillermo A. Sherwell
Gulielma Zollinger
Gustav Flaubert
H. A. Cody
H. B. Irving
H. C. Bailey
H. G. Wells
H. H. Munro
H. Irving Hancock
H. R. Naylor
H. Rider Haggard
H. W. C. Davis
Haldeman Julius
Hall Caine
Hamilton Wright Mabie
Hans Christian Andersen
Harold Avery
Harold McGrath
Harriet Beecher Stowe
Harry Castlemon
Harry Coghill
Harry Houidini

Hayden Carruth
Helent Hunt Jackson
Helen Nicolay
Hendrik Conscience
Hendy David Thoreau
Henri Barbusse
Henrik Ibsen
Henry Adams
Henry Ford
Henry Frost
Henry James
Henry Jones Ford
Henry Seton Merriman
Henry W Longfellow
Herbert A. Giles
Herbert Carter
Herbert N. Casson
Herman Hesse
Hildegard G. Frey
Homer
Honore De Balzac
Horace B. Day
Horace Walpole
Horatio Alger Jr.
Howard Pyle
Howard R. Garis
Hugh Lofting
Hugh Walpole
Humphry Ward
Ian Maclaren
Inez Haynes Gillmore
Irving Bacheller
Isabel Cecilia Williams
Isabel Hornibrook
Israel Abrahams
Ivan Turgenev
J. G.Austin
J. Henri Fabre
J. M. Barrie
J. M. Walsh
J. Macdonald Oxley
J. R. Miller
J. S. Fletcher
J. S. Knowles
J. Storer Clouston
J. W. Duffield
Jack London
Jacob Abbott
James Allen
James Andrews
James Baldwin

James Branch Cabell
James DeMille
James Joyce
James Lane Allen
James Lane Allen
James Oliver Curwood
James Oppenheim
James Otis
James R. Driscoll
Jane Abbott
Jane Austen
Jane L. Stewart
Janet Aldridge
Jens Peter Jacobsen
Jerome K. Jerome
Jessie Graham Flower
John Buchan
John Burroughs
John Cournos
John F. Kennedy
John Gay
John Glasworthy
John Habberton
John Joy Bell
John Kendrick Bangs
John Milton
John Philip Sousa
John Taintor Foote
Jonas Lauritz Idemil Lie
Jonathan Swift
Joseph A. Altsheler
Joseph Carey
Joseph Conrad
Joseph E. Badger Jr
Joseph Hergesheimer
Joseph Jacobs
Jules Vernes
Julian Hawthrone
Julie A Lippmann
Justin Huntly McCarthy
Kakuzo Okakura
Karle Wilson Baker
Kate Chopin
Kenneth Grahame
Kenneth McGaffey
Kate Langley Bosher
Kate Langley Bosher
Katherine Cecil Thurston
Katherine Stokes
L. A. Abbot
L. T. Meade

L. Frank Baum
Latta Griswold
Laura Dent Crane
Laura Lee Hope
Laurence Housman
Lawrence Beasley
Leo Tolstoy
Leonid Andreyev
Lewis Carroll
Lewis Sperry Chafer
Lilian Bell
Lloyd Osbourne
Louis Hughes
Louis Joseph Vance
Louis Tracy
Louisa May Alcott
Lucy Fitch Perkins
Lucy Maud Montgomery
Luther Benson
Lydia Miller Middleton
Lyndon Orr
M. Corvus
M. H. Adams
Margaret E. Sangster
Margret Howth
Margaret Vandercook
Margaret W. Hungerford
Margret Penrose
Maria Edgeworth
Maria Thompson Daviess
Mariano Azuela
Marion Polk Angellotti
Mark Overton
Mark Twain
Mary Austin
Mary Catherine Crowley
Mary Cole
Mary Hastings Bradley
Mary Roberts Rinehart
Mary Rowlandson
M. Wollstonecraft Shelley
Maud Lindsay
Max Beerbohm
Myra Kelly
Nathaniel Hawthrone
Nicolo Machiavelli
O. F. Walton
Oscar Wilde
Owen Johnson
P.G. Wodehouse
Paul and Mabel Thorne

Paul G. Tomlinson
Paul Severing
Percy Brebner
Percy Keese Fitzhugh
Peter B. Kyne
Plato
Quincy Allen
R. Derby Holmes
R. L. Stevenson
R. S. Ball
Rabindranath Tagore
Rahul Alvares
Ralph Bonehill
Ralph Henry Barbour
Ralph Victor
Ralph Waldo Emmerson
Rene Descartes
Ray Cummings
Rex Beach
Rex E. Beach
Richard Harding Davis
Richard Jefferies
Richard Le Gallienne
Robert Barr
Robert Frost
Robert Gordon Anderson
Robert L. Drake
Robert Lansing
Robert Lynd
Robert Michael Ballantyne
Robert W. Chambers
Rosa Nouchette Carey
Rudyard Kipling
Saint Augustine
Samuel B. Allison
Samuel Hopkins Adams
Sarah Bernhardt
Sarah C. Hallowell
Selma Lagerlof
Sherwood Anderson
Sigmund Freud
Standish O'Grady
Stanley Weyman
Stella Benson
Stella M. Francis
Stephen Crane
Stewart Edward White
Stijn Streuvels
Swami Abhedananda
Swami Parmananda
T. S. Ackland

T. S. Arthur
The Princess Der Ling
Thomas A. Janvier
Thomas A Kempis
Thomas Anderton
Thomas Bailey Aldrich
Thomas Bulfinch
Thomas De Quincey
Thomas Dixon
Thomas H. Huxley
Thomas Hardy
Thomas More
Thornton W. Burgess
U. S. Grant
Upton Sinclair
Valentine Williams
Various Authors
Vaughan Kester
Victor Appleton
Victor G. Durham
Victoria Cross
Virginia Woolf
Wadsworth Camp
Walter Camp
Walter Scott
Washington Irving
Wilbur Lawton
Wilkie Collins
Willa Cather
Willard F. Baker
William Dean Howells
William le Queux
W. Makepeace Thackeray
William W. Walter
William Shakespeare
Winston Churchill
Yei Theodora Ozaki
Yogi Ramacharaka
Young E. Allison
Zane Grey

www.ingramcontent.com/pod-product-compliance
Lightning Source LLC
Chambersburg PA
CBHW030130180626
46812CB00002B/637